By

D.T Burroughs

TABLE OF CONTENTS

One: Hunter Killer

With a grunt, Dan Harving pulled himself up to peer over the stony ledge. The cliff he clung to rose above a thick, pine forest. He held on with only one hand, for his other hand carried his pistol. He knew he should have holstered the firearm and kept three points of contact, but he was an experienced climber and with everything that had been happening recently, he felt safer with it drawn. The ledge he clung to pressed close against the tree line above it. As he crested the lip, he saw that there was only a few feet of bald land between the pines and the cliff. Looking around he didn't see anything out of the ordinary. The area above seemed safe. At least, that's how it seemed. One could never be too careful out in the wilds. He'd take it slow. With another grunt he hauled himself up and over, lugging his hundred and forty pound backpack and rifle over the ledge. He stood tall, at an imposing six nine and braced himself against the strong wind.

He kept his back to the cliff, ignoring the view. The scenery was a magnificent ocean of rolling mountains, each painted a rich, deep green. A powerful river raged below, and the sound of its roaring rapids continuously echoed off the stone faces of the gorge. The river was fed by a mighty waterfall that thundered in the distance, its waters clashed against rocks and churned up thick foam.

All of this was pushed out of Dan's mind. His senses reached out to pick at every little sound and movement from the old mountain forest. A breeze blew around him. It tousled his long, brown hair that grew down to his lower back and ruffled his chest long beard. This wind, however, brought something more with it. The pungent smell of death lingered in his nostrils. It was a new death; fresh, raw meat with a sour note of copper.

Holstering the sidearm, he unslung his rifle and knelt next to a trampled fern. After a moment of pawing around in the dirt he found what he was looking for. The imprint of a large human hand pressed into the softer soil around the plant. Following the direction of the print he could expertly discern the telltale signs of an animal pushing its way into the tree line. A pressed plant, a snapped branch, and a bent sapling was all he needed to follow.

Carefully, he stalked into the woods. The forest enveloped him and darkened the world till it was an eerie twilight. The noise from the thundering falls slowly faded away until the only sound was the occasional chirp of a bird and the slow, methodical crunch of the dried debris from the timbers under his gargantuan boots. The wind picked up again and brought with it the raw smell; powerful this time. He was close. Dan's steps became glacially slow and deliberate, like a big cat stalking its prey. As he approached a fallen tree, he made himself as low as possible, crouching down and hugging his knees as he continued to pad forward. As he peeked over the log he was met with a grizzly sight.

Dan was looking into a natural clearing with several boulders the size of small houses. Huge granite erratics were scattered throughout the clearing. The sides of the enormous stones were plastered with blood; some of it even looked intentional. There were shapes that looked like they were drawn with naked hands, as if a morbid child had finger-painted the stones.

Blocky, simplified depictions showed nightmarish illustrations of a strange, yellow disk stealing children in the night, of cracking men's heads with rocks, of dismembering large cats in the woods. Like graffiti on a wall, the pictures were sporadically tagged, and buzzing around the scenes of violence were strange squiggles and shapes.

The lines were smeared onto the stone, and as they traveled along, the lines broke, fused, and turned at strangely precise geometric angles. Some of the lines that broke away traveled in their own, strange and angular branches until they ended with a sharp slash.

The rest of the glade was awash with splashes of red and liberally speckled with chunks of meat. The deafening buzzing of flies was the only sound to be heard as he sat and observed for several minutes.

Whatever had done this seemed to have gone. He tentatively stepped into the clearing and investigated. Dan knelt down next to the body. Was this the cougar he had tagged? Yes, it had to be... he could tell by its paws. The paws were just about the only parts that were not pulped, shredded, or gnawed to ribbons.

Although he had smelled it from far off, he had hoped it was natural predation, but this was something else. By the gore on it, he could tell a heavy stone was used to break the long bones so the marrow could be gotten at. A crude stone knife lay next to the body, along with a large stone. By the splatter, he guessed the stone had been used to tenderize the meat, or maybe whatever had done this was just playing in the gore.

While he surveyed the area, he heard a small wisp of sand and pebbles sprinkle down from one of the large boulders behind him. On edge, he whirled around, rifle ready. On top of the rocks stood... something. It looked familiar, but his vision seemed to blur around the figure. It stood silhouetted against the sky, making him unable to focus on it clearly.

The thing's aura bore down on his psyche as an unnatural and foreign fear surged through him. This was a fear like he'd never known. In his time, he'd tracked apex predators, broken bones in the wild, been shot at by poachers, and been lost for weeks away from civilization. Dan knew how to handle fear, but this panic cut him to his core. Until now he had only swum in pools and lakes of fear, but now he swam in an ocean of it. The strange being that stood before him was like a wave that rose up taller than a mountain. It would crash down and crush him into the depths of blackness; the kind that only the mad could ever glimpse. For a moment it petrified him, but his body reacted on muscle memory, shouldering the rifle while his mind balked.

Dan tried to aim, but the world seemed to spin before him. A dizzying array of half formed pictures – twisting, unfocused and without color. Relying on muscle memory alone he pulled the trigger, then grabbed the bolt and forced it back to eject the case and load the next shot. He repeated this again and again and again; each time operating the rifle's bolt action with the skill he'd refined over his entire life.

Then there was no more. He had emptied his rifle and the thing still stood; its shadowy form delineated against the dark clouds. Impossible. He looked down and saw a pile of bullets. Not empty shells, not shell casings, just unspent bullets. He had ejected unfired ammunition. Every. Single. Shot.

Confusion and horror gripped his heart as he tried to look back at the thing, but it was becoming hard to stand. All he could see as he tried to stay on his feet was a warm, gently glowing, yellow orb against the rain heavy sky.

Two: Homecoming

Dear Mr. Jones,

"Thank you for showing interest in our company. Unfortunately,-"

Jay deleted the email from his phone and scrolled to the next one on the short list of replies he'd gotten that day.

"We're afraid that-"

Delete.

"We regret to inform you that because of your record, we're unable to offer you-"

Delete.

Delete.

Delete.

Delete.

"God fucking *damn it!*" he shouted. With a roar of anger Jay threw his phone into the couch cushions. He flopped down next to it and hung his head, running his fingers over his prickly short hair. He tried to calm down, he really did. He tried to breathe. He tried to focus on his goals and everything else the therapist told him to do, but his thoughts were hooked deep, hung upon his rejection. He began to spiral down into the darkness of his own mind. He dug his fingers into his scalp, feeling the bald line of a scar healed long ago as he screamed. He shrieked at the world like a banshee until his throat hurt and tears blurred his sight. His pale skin glowed red from the rage, the helplessness, and the hopelessness that overtook him.

A fist banged against the other side of his living room wall. From the next apartment over, a muffled shout came through, "Hey!" they barked, "shut the fuck up or I'll bust your god damn teeth in!"

5

Jay sneered at the wall, but he took a deep breath trying to steady and compose himself. Then there was a small stinging on his arm. He scratched it and a flea shot off, escaping with his blood. He continued to scratch the spot, then stopped, looking at his arm contemplatively. He stood up and crossed the room to take a look at himself in the tall mirror. It had been there when he moved in, just hanging on the wall. It had a large, jagged crack down the middle, but since it still worked, he had decided to keep it. He lifted his shirt and glared with contempt at the bag of bones he saw reflecting back at him. He'd become a shadow of the man he used to be. He was never a big guy, but now he could clearly see his ribs under his stretched skin. He did a little twist and found he could see his hips and spine too.

After a few moments he couldn't look any longer and cast his gaze around the room. It was a ground floor studio apartment. The walls were stained with grease, dirt and... something else. He wondered if any CSI team had ever been in here. The entire room smelled like a combination of stale ramen noodles, sweat, urine, and who knew what else. The carpet was likewise stained with a variety of brown, black, and other undescriptive colors. He could tell these were different from those on the wall because they were stickier and the smell was far worse. The paint on the cabinets in the kitchen was peeling and just as bad as anything else in the apartment. He hoped it wasn't from someone cooking meth; not that he had many housing options other than here. Just then, a roach crawled out from under the couch. Jay quickly grabbed the empty ashtray from the rented particle board coffee table and crushed it. One more stain. At least he knew what this one was.

There had to be a way out. First, he needed to take stock of what resources he had on hand, so Jay emptied his wallet out onto the coffee table. Twenty three dollars and some odd cents. After shuffling through some loose papers, he found what he was looking for and picked up the Past Due letter. Eight hundred dollars. Eight hundred a month for this cesspit; and this was one of the cheap ones.

All he could do was just sit there, eyeing the letter like it had kicked his dog. His vision began to go blurry again, so he blinked it away, cleared his throat and went to the fridge. It was a dull, off white, wasteland filled to the brim with a whole lot of nothing, save for a jar of mayonnaise, some discounted lunch meat, and a jug of water. He didn't trust the pipes. He pulled out the meat and opened the package. To his disgust, he found the thin slices were polka dotted with green, fuzzy circles. He threw the package of meat into the trash with a disheartened sigh. Looking between the jar and the jug, Jay sighed deeply once again and gave a "fuck it" shrug. With the jar and a spoon in hand, he flopped despondently back onto the couch.

With the exception of some stale fries he'd salvaged out of a trash can, he hadn't eaten that day. As such, the first spoonful was a punch to his senses. It was a tangy tragedy of a morsel and unreasonably tart. It was so sour that it made him grimace and pucker. As he forced himself to swallow the disastrous contents, he reflexively gagged as it hit the back of his throat. Forcing back his body's urge to reject the stuff, he managed to down the first bite. The second was no more pleasant, but it wasn't necessarily worse as his pallet became accustomed to the abuse.

Several bites into his meal, Jay felt a rumbling underneath him. Deciding that it was probably just another rejection email he continued to force another spoonful down his throat. The phone rumbled again, then after a pause a third time. Someone was calling him. Maybe for an interview! He frantically stuffed his hand between the cushions and fished out his phone. With electric excitement he managed to fat thumb the talk button and splutter out, "Hello?"

"Hello, is this Josiah Jones?" the voice on the other end inquired in a professional tone.

Jay's heart soared as he set the jar off to the side and scrambled for a pen and paper. "Yes, this is him," he replied, forcing his voice to contain his excitement.

"Jay! Holy shit, man. How you doin'? It's Mathew!"

Jay's brain locked up as it tried to shift gears from a job interview to "who the hell is this". While his brain turned over, all he could blurt out was a dull, "Uh, yeah, I'm doin' good."

7

"Good to hear, man. Hey, what are you up to right now?"

With disdain, he looked at the jar and spoon on the coffee table. "Just sittin' down for dinner." It was at that moment that his brain caught up with him. "Wait, Mat? Mat Gerhard?"

"Hell yeah, man!"

"Shit, brother, I ain't seen you since freshman year. How's the great 'ol northwest treatin' ya?"

"Pretty damn fine, actually. If nothin' else it beats sweating your balls off in the Texas summer."

"Ha! *Your* balls, maybe. Why don' you come on home and see if you don' fall in love with it all over again?"

"Funny you should say that, man, I'm actually in town visiting my mom."

"Oh yeah?"

"Yeah, man. I'm heading out tomorrow. I know you just sat down, but I was wonderin' if you wanted to grab a burger and beer. My treat."

Jay looked over at the repulsive jar of sour ooze and without hesitating said, "Hell yeah, brother."

"And maybe I can finally collect on our bet. You still owe me four dollars-"

"-and forty five cents," Jay interrupted with a chuckle, "damn it, you're still doggin' me about that? I told you I'd get you back when my dadd'eh paid me."

With a warm chuckle Mat responded, "See you soon, man."

– – – – – – – – –

Jay stepped into the bar and looked around. The light was dim and warm. The long, wrap-around bar had a shiny oak countertop, and was seated with stools that had tall, wooden legs and smooth, worn seats which any man could slide into after a long day. The sound of cracking pool balls briefly interrupted the T.V. A sports broadcaster was breaking down the play by play of the latest football game. The Somebodies beat the Whoevers, and it was the best-est thing ever. Jay didn't dislike the game, he just didn't have the zeal that everyone else in, literally, the entire state had for it. That meant, of course, that he was a witch and wished a pox on anyone who enjoyed it, and that he should be crucified for his heretical beliefs.

Jay was thankfully pulled away from his thoughts by a friendly "Hey, man". Mat was sitting at a table in the corner and waving him over. The big man stood up and greeted him with a bone splintering hug that lifted Jay's feet off the floor. Jay had always been a bit on the shorter side and Mat was a veritable giant. Mat's natural and honed athleticism did no favors for Jay's struggling lungs as he tried to wriggle out of the embrace. Mat had played football in middle school and damn near lived in the school gym. He would have made quarterback if he wasn't black. That brought back fond memories of the two of them egging the coaches house and car; and head. Mat finally, mercifully, saw fit to put his friend down and let him breathe.

They sat back down at the table, which was trickier for Jay as he had to climb up into the chair. It was a standing table with chairs that had legs like a giraffe. A single, dim, triangular light hung over the table to illuminate their little corner. Mat had already ordered, and a hot burger with all the fixings sat next to a dripping cold beer; dark and rich.

Jay was about to dig in, but kept looking over his shoulder and fidgeted in his chair. "I hate to be a princess 'bout this," he said, "but can we swap chairs? I got this thing 'bout my back bein' out."

With a shrug, Mat just said, "Sure, man."

They swapped seats, and after mounting the giraffe-like chair again, Jay had his back safely against the wall. With ravenous zeal, he grabbed the greasy burger, chomped several mouthfuls, and then washed it all down with a long swig of beer. It was perfect. A touch of char around the edges, pink in the middle... and no fucking mayo! Each bite chased down with cold, rich, foaming honey colored beer. Pure ambrosia! This was *the* best thing in the whole damn world.

Mat chuckled and pushed over a basket of loaded Texas fries. "Like a man out of the desert."

Jay waved an apology as he wolfed down the huge bite of food he had bitten off. "Best damn thing I had'n a long time."

Mat picked up his burger and before taking a bite asked, "By the way, what the hell happened to that glorious lion's mane of yours?"

Rubbing his short head of hair Jay laughed and said, "Yeah, I cut that quite a while back, now. I see you lost your fro."

His reply came through a mouthful of food, "It waff not a damn fro."

With a mischievous smile Jay said, "If you can hide three pencils, an eraser, and a sharpener in it, it's a fro."

They laughed into a comfortable silence of eating and drinking. After a while Mat perked up and asked, "How's your dad doin' these days?"

"Dead, finally."

"Shit, man. I knew he was a hard ass, but damn."

"Well your ass don't have switch scars, so you can mourn 'im all you like. How's your mama doin'?"

"She's good; doin' good. She just got done with her last round of chemo."

"Oh shit! Mary got cancer?"

"Yup, yup. Found it early on, on a routine, um, exam," Mat said as he awkwardly waved his hand in front of his chest, "s'why I'm in town, actually."

"Checkin' in on 'er?"

Mat rolled his eyes and leaned back in his chair, throwing his hands up in defeat. "Yes! That stubborn ass woman. She calls me up and is all, 'Hey, baby boy, I love you, your sister's good, your cousin's got new jobs, and oh yeah, *I beat cancer*. How're you?'"

Jay burst out laughing and shook his head. "Damn, 'tween Mary and the cancer I feel bad for the cancer; poor thing never stood a *chance* 'gainst *her*."

The two fell into another comfortable silence while they enjoyed their meal. Then after a short time of reading the subtitles on the television and wolfing down the burger and beer – serenaded with a few deep and satisfying belches, Jay slowed and thought to himself. His brow furrowed as he tried to puzzle something out. Eventually he gave up and just asked.

"Hey, Mat, How'd you get my number, anyhow? Don' think I've had this damn thing 'more than a few months, and I di'n give it out all willy nilly."

Mat was happily chewing, but sobered at the question. He swallowed, looked at his friend and shrugged. "You know better'n that, small town living, everyone knows everyone's business."

Jay put his beer down and gave it a thousand-yard stare. "So you heard?"

"I heard, but I couldn't believe it till I called your jail. I spoke to the warden, direct."

"So, you know what I done," Jay could feel a lump rising in his throat, only held down by his sinking shame.

"Only what's on the public record, but I want to hear it from you. What the hell, man?"

Jay sighed and leaned over his beer with down cast eyes and a low voice, "Well, like you said, it's a small town. You're in school, some bastard thinks he's hot shit, so you gotta learn the little fucker some manners. Little shit don' learn an' grows up to be a big shit. Well, there ain't that many jobs, and all the shops are family owned so the little shit and all his friends end up owning all the business. They burn your name 'round town, an' of course your

11

daddy drank all the money. You ain't got grades for much, so you get it in your fool head to rob a bank. Flash a gun, everyone lays down, you get a sack of cash big enough to get out; go make somethin' of yourself. Plus, banks are insured by the government so it's just 'bout a victimless crime."

After a pause and a long sigh, Jay continued, "Then some fat, sweaty man-cow gets it in his fool head that he's gonna be some big damn hero. Daddy din' teach me much, but he said, 'Never get a gun, 'les you're 'pared 't use it'. Maybe it wasn't that useful of advice after all."

"So, I stay and try to stop the bleeding, the police come and take me in. The man-cow dies in the hospital, then I have to listen to his heffer of a mother berate me in court 'bout how I, 'took her baby,' an' how much he loved them foreign cartoons with the big eyes; and how he was gonna make 'em someday."

Jay sighed and drained his beer. "But she's right. So, I did my time, kept my head down and my nose clean... s'much as you can when you're caged with a bunch of crazies. 'Least with animals you know where you stand, but crazies? They'd kill you as soon as they'd look at you."

All Mat could say was a quiet, "Shit, man."

They sat in silence for a long while, watching the game, neither one really paying attention. The two were snapped back when someone scored, and the crowd cheered.

Mat crossed his giant arms and sat back in his chair, his head tilted to one side, and thought for a minute. An awkward silence fell upon the table, neither one speaking, or even looking at each other. Finally, it was Mat that broke the silence, though the question didn't help the awkwardness. "You shank anybody in there?"

Jay fidgeted with his empty bottle. "You do what you have to in there."

"Where the hell do you even get a knife in prison?"

"Bribe somebody, or buy it, or trade off another guy, or it gets slipped in for you. I made mine. You can make fuckin' shank out of anything if you got to. Fucking prison arts and crafts!"

"Out of what? A sharpened toothbrush?" Mat asked in a disbelieving tone, "you ain't owned a toothbrush since middle school!"

They both laughed off the ribbing. Just like back in the day. Jay smiled and said, "Nah, toilet paper and glue in Art Therapy." Matt busted out a laugh, but wasn't sure if Jay was telling the truth or bullshitting.

Mat then scoffed and finished his beer. "Ok, MacGyver. Who'd you end up having to... you know?"

Jay leaned back and thought for a moment. "A Nazi and his two friends, a black fella who wanted to bust my head open for looking at him wrong, and a Mexican who was as skinny as he was crazy. If I'da got a chinaman, I'da got the whole set."

At that, Mat had to laugh, caught off guard by the dark humor, and only finished chuckling several moments later with an amused smile. The smile slowly faded as he became lost in thought.

After several minutes Mat nodded to himself and said flatly, "It's yours, if you want it."

Jay stopped rolling his bottle around and looked at his friend, confused. "What, your virginity?"

Mat flipped him off with a smile. "Naw, bro. A job."

"A handy? Blowy? Rim?"

"A lumber job," he said flat out.

"Is that what the kids are calling it these days?"

"Damn it, Jay, I'm serious. I own a logging company and we help a lot of convicts get on their feet. With a felony under your belt I can't imagine your prospects have got much better."

Jay just sat and rolled his bottle some more. "Truth be told, nothin's changed. I hit a snag tryin' to get my life together, and I'm still hurtin' for money. I still want out, and that bank was lookin' mighty tempting, not gonna lie." With the empty beer in hand, he raised a toast. "I'll take it, but why even bother? I fucked up more than a man can fix."

He was met with a sad look. "Because you're my friend. After I found out, I had to look you in the eye. I had to see with my own eyes if you were still in there; you're still my friend, Jay. And lucky you, we had a guy quit about a month back. Just left camp without saying a word. So," Mat clapped his hands together, "I'll get you a written copy of our training before I leave so you have something to do on your flight. Then, once you get there we can jump right into the onsite training."

Jay looked up at his friend nervously. In a sheepish voice he said, "I ain't got no money for a ticket, or anything else really."

Mat pulled out a check book and began scribbling. "Ok, this'll be a business loan for travel expenses. Save all your receipts, and you can give back what you don't spend. What you *do* spend can be taken out of your first paycheck."

Jay watched his friend scribble for a moment. His first thought was to tell him he couldn't take his money, or say he wasn't worth it, but another thought rang a little louder. "You're gonna smack me if I refuse this, ain't you?"

"Damn right I am!" he said as he cut the check and handed it over.

Jay had to roll his head back and sniff back a tear, but managed to grunt, "Thanks, brother."

"Don't get all emotional. It's good to have you back." Mat walked over to the bar and paid the tab. He turned back to Jay with a warm smile as he said, "Have a good night, man. I'll get those papers to you in the morning." With a wave, Mat began to walk toward the door.

Before he stepped out, Jay had a mischievous little thought. He knew he probably shouldn't, but he just couldn't help himself. He called out to his friend, "Hey, Mat."

Mat turned to see his friend suggestively stroking the neck of the beer bottle while he cocked an eyebrow up, an impish grin plastered across his face.

Mat laughed and shook his head. With an amused snort, he mustered a simple, "Fuck you."

Three: New Beginnings

The old doors of the bus creaked as they opened. Jay hiked up his backpack with one arm, and in the other he held the binder full of his future. He was able to fit his whole life into a backpack, so he didn't have any luggage to put under the bus. The upside to traveling so light was that he was one of the first to board so he decided to take a seat near the front where he could put his back firmly against the window. This meant he could watch people get on and relax a little. Jay was glad to be out of the station. It was in the bad part of town. The little corner of the county, like so many others, that had been economically neglected for years, just like the forgotten people who lived in it.

Now that he'd boarded, he didn't really know what to do with himself, so he just stared out the window across from him and absent mindedly drummed on his knees. There was a little fluttering in his chest; a sensation he couldn't remember ever feeling. It was similar to the panic he had felt when he knew he'd be going to prison, only this time it felt lighter. The sensation before was like a weighted, sinking feeling of doom that threatened to crush him flat, but this felt almost inspiring. Was this what hope felt like? Fear of the unknown mixed a wish that it would be ok?

Deciding that he needed to keep his mind busy, he opened up the binder. It was a cheap, white, 3-ring plastic binder. Probably half of its contents would describe how to not die on the clock; safety first, and all that. The other half would be about laws and regulations. It was going to be the driest reading material ever penned to paper, but it would pass the time.

Eventually the passengers loaded, found their seats and the bus started up with a diesel roar, turning his seat into a discount massage chair. As the metal tube pulled out of the station, Jay took one last look at the only place he'd ever known. A little smile found its way onto his lips as he pressed his middle finger to the glass.

– – – – – – – – –

The legalese of his binder was so dry, he'd spent more time trying not to fall asleep than he had reading. Several pages were read so mechanically that Jay couldn't recall a single thing about them. Taking a breath and rolling his head back, he stared at the ceiling with half lidded eyes. If he'd had to read while locked up, maybe he would have been able to sleep better. He had always had trouble learning like this. The tedium of sitting and having your world shrink to some boring, coarse, white paper and a never-ending cluster of black squiggles. Where was the excitement? Where were the pictures? After giving the topic some further thought, he realized that whenever something *did* stick, it was usually because it was interesting; or funny, or when he was talking with someone instead of reading it. Jay let out a mischievous little chuckle as he recalled one of his favorite, and least mature, factoids about how the moon landing took place in 1969. *That* fact had stayed with him the second he'd learned it.

With a drowsy yawn he looked out the window. The sun was already below the horizon, with its last tendrils of light peeking over the world. The horizon line was a brilliant red and orange mixture that gently gave way to yellow. As the yellow rose up it slowly smeared into a dull green which, in turn, smeared into blue, like an upside-down rainbow. Looking straight up, the sky had a long, dark purple band that separated the blue from the black. Out from the black, the stars were beginning to shine. Jay took it as a sign he should probably bed down. He hadn't accomplished much reading, but it was exhausting, nonetheless. So with his backpack as a pillow, he propped his head up, and in lieu of a blanket or coat he hugged himself. As he shut his eyes, he let the rumble of the bus lull him to sleep.

— — — — — — — — — —

Jay rubbed his eyes with his fists, took a deep breath and gazed out the window. The scenery whizzed by and swirled like a watercolor painting. There wasn't much to look at this far out, anyway. It was all flat, dry, and boring. Almost unnaturally flat, it seemed. It had been like this for a few days now. From horizon to horizon there was just featureless land. To Jay, it was like the land that creation forgot. It seemed like it was a smooth, concrete foundation for a building the size of the whole world, but the building never got built. The whole thing felt like purgatory, and it made him uneasy.

He put his binder on his seat and stood up. He needed to drain the lizard. Supporting himself on the seats, he moved to the back of the bus. As he reached the back, he smiled at a beautiful young mother and her little girl. The girl was crouched between the seats and was putting her fingers through the grate of a cat carrier. She pet the little critter with her finger tips while she whispered little assurances to it.

With an amused chuckle, he entered the bathroom and did his business, washed up, and returned to his seat. Once he flopped back down, he dove back into the safety, rules, regulations, and "regulatory compliance" issues of logging until the next stop.

The bus pulled into the station and everyone got off. Some transferred, some just went to stretch their legs, and some scrambled to desecrate a bathroom that they *wouldn't* be trapped next to for hours on end.

Jay got a premade sandwich, a coffee, some snacks, and a breath of fresh air. Sitting outside on a bench against the wall of the station, he enjoyed the sunshine and his humble meal – which was still better than what he was used to lately. He topped his sandwich with the salty chips to give it the perfect crunch. Once he'd taken his first bite, he practically inhaled the sandwich, not realizing how hungry he'd been. Feeling more content now, he opened the bag of peanut butter mini cookies and blissfully dunked them into his coffee.

While he contently munched on his treat he saw the little girl and her mother again. The big orange cat, now freed from the confinement of its crate, was on a harness and tentatively sniffing every blade of grass. It stepped gingerly through the lawn until it found a suitable place to do its business. The cat prowled around for a while longer while Jay finished up. With a little knowing smile, appreciating the cat's freedom, he threw his garbage in the trash and went back to the bus.

He was relaxing in his front row seat as people began to trickle back on. The girl came back, practically dragging the struggling cat behind her. The scene got an amused little chuckle out of Jay. That thing did *not* want to go back to its cage; and he could relate. She managed to wrangle it back to her seat and began to try and gently push the animal back into its carrier. The cat was having none of it.

It began to wriggle, and wrestle, and squirm. Jay leaned forward into the open aisle. The closer it was shoved toward the door, the more desperately it fought. Then the little girl screamed as the cat twisted and dug its claws into her. It kicked off in a panicked bid for freedom, fleeing like she'd been trying to drown it.

It landed at a dead sprint and surged toward the open doors. The orange blur shot past the mother who had come running at her child's scream. It dashed down the aisle until it was just one more panicked leap to freedom.

Then suddenly a hand shot out and pinned the cat to the ground. With a firm grip on the scruff of its neck, Jay lifted the cat and cradled its hind legs to take some of the pull off its neck. Triumphantly, he walked back to the girl and put the cat deep into the carrier, then quickly shut the door after letting go. "I know buddy, I know," he murmured.

The mother tucked the cat away and smiled up at Jay. "Thank you so much, I don't know what we'd have done if we had lost him." She hugged her daughter and affectionately rubbed the little girl's head. "She can't stand being away from her little Tiger."

"Is she alright?" he inquired.

"Oh, yes. I think it scared her more than anything. There are some red spots, but no blood." She gently nudged the little girl and whispered, "What do we say, Cynthia?"

The little girl looked sheepishly at Jay's feet and said, "Thank you, mister sir." Then she frowned at the crate and smacked the top of it with her little hand. "*Bad* Tiger."

Jay smiled and knelt down. "Oh, now, Tiger ain't bad. He's just scared. He don't know what's going on, and little kitties don't like cages, even if they need 'em sometimes. I'm sure he's real sorry he scared you, an' as soon as you get to where you're goin', he'll give you a nice big hug and a kiss on your nose. Careful he don't lick it off, now. New noses are hard to come by."

The little girl giggled. "Noses don't come off." Then her smile faded and she looked worried. "Did you hurt Tiger when you grabbed him?"

"No, no, he ain't hurt none. When momma kitties pick up their babies they pick them up with their mouths, right on the back of the neck. They got extra skin there so it don't hurt none, and it makes them go limp so's they don't get hurt by momma's teeth. Big 'ol boys like him still do the same thing."

"So he's ok?"

"Oh yeah, darlin'. Didn't hurt him a bit."

She smiled and scrambled down to pet the cat through the holes.

The mother put out her slender hand to shake his. "Thank you again, mister...?"

Shaking her hand gently, he smiled and said, "Just Jay's fine, ma'am."

"Melanie. So, Mister Jay, do you have far to go?"

Four: A Strange New World

Her little hand waved furiously as the bus pulled away, leaving the little family at their station. Jay waved back at the pair until they were out of sight. A gentle smile broke his lips as he leaned back into the seat, and felt the rumblings of the big diesel engine. He closed his eyes and rested, contemplating how much he'd enjoyed the last few days. He'd lost track of how many had gone by. Melanie understood some legalese, and was able to talk him through the more complicated bits of his binder. The terminology and corporate speak bored him to tears, but she made it manageable. Afterward, they just shot the breeze until it was time for her stop. It was good. He literally couldn't remember the last time he'd spent a whole day in conversation, let alone several. It was probably with Mat, back when they were kids. They'd been inseparable back then. Either way, it was good. With his work complete, and his day well spent, he let himself get rocked into a comfortable sleep.

He was back at the bus stop, having lunch while a big orange cat sat on his head. He reached up and the cat leapt off before he could catch it. He got up to go after it, but the cat was fast and it felt as if he were running through water. Every movement he made was labored and strenuous, but he pressed on and chased the tiger into the woods anyway.

Then he felt something shift in the dreamscape. Nothing specific, but the texture of the dream seemed to have altered somehow. He was in the middle of a forest now, but nothing like the forests he was used to. Where he grew up, the leaves changed colors as the months passed throughout the year. He was from a land where the trees were thinner, sprinkled all through the land along with a handful of shrubs and bushes. This place was thick with nature, like a jungle; a Pacific Northwest rainforest. The foliage was so dense he couldn't see more than thirty feet in any direction. Plants covered the world at every height, from ferns on the ground, to bushes taller than a man, to trees that rose up over six stories tall.

The tiger appeared at his feet. It was only about the size of a kitten, but the vicious predator grappled his ankle and attempted to devour it. Jay bent down and put the little feline into the pocket of his jeans.

Once it settled in his pocket, a strange sound crept through his ears. It was like an undulating, high pitched squeal that came from deeper in the woods. A thin mist began to curl between the pines, illuminating the dim forest in an eerie blue light. He followed the sound, lured toward its haunting notes like a siren's song. He snuck over a fallen tree and peeked into a clearing. It was littered with boulders the size of small houses, rising up like some sort of ancient henge. The boulders bore illustrations, sloppily painted with shapes, lines and symbols, all illustrated in some blackish-red media. In the center of the strange henge stood a large deer, a stag. With its mouth opened wide, it called out. From deep within its throat, a preternatural sound erupted. From its lips the deer released a horrid screeching like that of an elk who swallowed a screaming table saw. A high pitched, piercing wail that lowered into a deep throated, contrabass grunt.

He knew it was wrong, even more wrong than it appeared, but he still stood transfixed. The stag was facing away from him and seemed unaware of his presence while it bleated and wailed. He was certain it didn't notice him, but he wasn't sure how he knew. It was a strange certainty, but certain he was. The bizarre creature continued to call, making him more uneasy with each husky shriek. Then he remembered the knife in his pocket. Looking down he slowly took it out. The knife had a tiger print handle and it felt good in his hand. It made him feel calmer, in control.

He was ready to face it now. Slowly, Jay rose and looked back over the log, but once he crested the timber, he felt his heart stop with surprise and terror. The stag stood directly in front of him, stretching its long neck over the log to shove its muzzle mere inches from his face. It stood massive, imposing, and tall; taller than him by far. Its imposing presence pressed down upon him like an extreme gravity. The lips peeled back and the jaw opened wide to reveal a maw littered with sharp, triangular canines. It possessed two eyes where one would expect, and in the center of its forehead rested a third. They bulged with sickly yellow pupils surrounded by piercing

24

white sclera. The thing let out its unearthly, banshee wail as it screamed directly in his face. The hot, foul smelling air curled around his nostrils and caressed his cheeks.

"Mister."

The ribs on its muscular body expanded as it sucked in a breath for another shrill tremor, yellow eyes burning into him; into *his mind*.

"Hey! You alright?"

A voice from above, from outside. A dream. Jay bolted awake. He was sweating and could feel his heart surging in his chest. Panting and wide eyed he frantically looked around.

A worry eyed stranger had nudged him out of his nightmare. "You were yelling and moaning; thought you might need some help." The stranger gave him a shy smile and walked off the bus.

Jay looked out the window to see the world had changed. The flat golden grasslands had given way to an endless expanse of rolling mountains that were covered in thick, green pines, like a million little hairs on the heads of giants. Mountain after mountain rolled off toward the horizon until all he could see in the distance was a snow peaked mountain with a flat top. It stood wide and solid, like a great defender ready to block what may come.

They had stopped off in a sleepy little town, Splitter Junction; population, nothing. It reminded him of home in that regard. He departed the bus, and decided to walk the little town. All the buildings were squat little single stories, just small Mom and Pop stores that were littered up and down the main street; which was really the only street to speak of. Unpaved streets branched off at odd angles down country roads where houses sat comfortably, nestled back deep into the woods. He walked by a knick knack shop, a salon, a pawn shop, and a handful of dive bars. There was even an inn that was made up to look all olde timey; or maybe it actually was olde timey. He half expected it to be called 'Ye Ol'… something'.

He stopped to peek through the window of the last store he passed and noticed a missing cat poster pinned to the wall next to it; poor thing. He hoped its owners were able to find it. Continuing up the road was an old fashioned burger and malt shop straight out of the fifties, a surprisingly modern looking building with travel info and pictures of hikers, another bar or two, and a grocery store that had a cork board on its wall outside. Several missing dog and cat posters decorated the board. He supposed that was common, living this close to the wilderness. Coyotes and bobcats, he guessed. One man had apparently even lost his hog. Judging from its picture, it was an impressively sized hog, too. Ok, that one would have to be a cougar, too big for a coyote or bobcat. He knew better, but he still hoped the pets were just lost.

Looking around, the tiny little town seemed perfect for someone who enjoyed a slower lifestyle. As he walked away from the board, a thought occurred. He'd have to ask somebody about what to look out for around here, predator wise. Thinking about a section in his binder, about how over logging could force predators closer to populated areas. There was an entire section about environmental regulations and impacts on wildlife and conservation efforts, and sustainable yadda yadda yadda.

Looking around, Jay noticed something odd. Most of the shops were closed, even though it was the middle of the day on a Saturday. To add more to the mystery, there didn't seem to be a single soul around; save for the shady young couple he'd passed, who wore too much black and dyed their hair purple. After turning a bend in the road, he found his answer. A large crowd of people were gathered at the end of the street. He decided to mosey on over and see what the hubbub was about.

A uniformed policeman in a bright green visibility vest stood on a little podium in the middle of the crowd, "-And stay in sight of the people to your left and to your right. Remember to use his name, he may be in an altered state of mind, so hearing his name will help him register what's happening." The officer continued talking but was drowned out momentarily by a passing red and white rescue helicopter.

The crowd began splitting into groups as Jay's stomach decided to speak up. He spied a little corner store with an old fashioned, wood carved "OPEN" sign hanging in the window. As he stepped through the door the little brass bell chimed and clattered. The one word that could be used to describe the store was simply, rustic. Charming rustic, or mountain murderer rustic, it was too soon to tell.

Sunlight lazily drizzled in through the dust painted windows of the quiet little shop. The metal frames of the shelving were made from thick, wrought iron from before machines mass produced everything. A fine layer of dust coated the wooden shelves and their contents all throughout the store, the selection of which was all fairly standard. Cans of soup, vegetables, and fruits, but mostly there were beans. Further down were boxes of off brand cereals, and towards the counter there was a psychedelic slurry of candy packaging. Some of the storage spaces were cozy recesses built into the walls themselves with the odd spider web here and there. All the other shelves were littered with little odds and ends, like pottery clearly made in town, or oil lanterns and jars of spices. It felt like walking into a grocery back in the old west, except for the technicolor packaging for the candy.

Walking around, Jay heard each footstep making the floorboards creak and groan. Taking a peek toward the back he saw barrels filled with strange farm tools or bags of feed. He liked the feel of the place, but he was here for a different kind of feed, so he went back to the front and looked over the small, refrigerated section.

Jay opened the door and scanned the row of sandwiches. Egg salad? No, too much mayo. He instead grabbed a turkey sandwich, checked the expiration date to make sure it was still good, and snagged a bag of chips, along with a bag of cookies, and a little glass bottle of orange juice. Jay made his way to the counter and greeted the elderly man who was reading a newspaper. The man had been peering at him over the top of it, eyeing him with a cautious but friendly smile. "Anything else for you today son?"

Son? Jay did not like being called 'son' but turnabout is fair play. "Howdy! No thanks Pops. Just this today."

The old man rang up the items and said, "That will be $9.50."

As the old man opened the register to get his change, Jay's eyes wandered behind the elderly cashier. He spied an old, worn and sun faded poster of the same snow topped mountain he had seen entering town. This one, however, looked like it had swallowed an apocalypse and was belching out doomsday. The amount of ash that erupted into the heavens dwarfed the mountain itself. Jay pointed at the poster and casually asked, "What's going on there?"

The old man turned and looked, "Oh, that's Mount Saint Helens. It blew its top back on May 18th 1980. Blew ash all the way to the east coast. We were buried up to our necks in the stuff."

"That much? Must've been like shovelin' the worst kind of snow, I'd imagine."

"Oh, it was dreadful. Yup, this whole place got buried good and deep, but it all worked out in the end. Way, way back before people moved here, this whole place had lava running through it, like veins in your arm. When the lava drained out it left all these caves. When we were digging ourselves out of the ash, a lot of them got dug up. My granddaughter loves all that cave exploring stuff. That's her there." He motioned towards a wall full of pictures of a young, beautiful woman decked out in climbing gear with lights on the helmet. Selfies outside caves, selfies inside caves, selfies of friends repelling down from rocks, chin deep in water pics. The thought of it gave Jay the creeps.

The proud old man continued, "She started telling her cave buddies and before we knew it, people from all over the world were coming here to explore. They call it slunkering or something like that. I've lived here all my life and we're doing better now than we ever have. Why, just the other day I had a man in here all the way from Japan. Said he'd been caving all over the world. I guess you could say that mountain blowing was good for us." The old man bagged the items and put them on the counter before he continued to drone on, "My wife loves all the people coming through. She used to travel all around, back in the day, but she doesn't travel much anymore; not since she got her hip replaced. She had to go all the way to the big city for that one, but she loves to get to talking to all the different people about where they're from. That Japanese fellow, I thought she'd talk his little yellow ears off."

28

Jay cleared his throat, a little put off by the sudden casual racism. Who knew small talk could get so big? He paid for his things and was about to walk out the door when he was reminded of the crowd. He knew he'd probably regret asking, but curiosity got the better of him. "Say, what's all the ruckus about out there?"

"Oh, terrible, that. A man's gone missing. Dan Harving. He was a local, he'd lived here for a few good years now. He was a government man. Big mountain of a fellow. He'd come in for supplies and we'd get to talking. Dan tracked cougars out there to keep an eye on their numbers, make sure there weren't too many, and such. It's a funny thing, he'd make sure there weren't too few, either. Too few and there's too many deer eating everything. Man had quite the history. He tracked Alaskan browns for about ten years; man knows his stuff. Last few years he's been watching the wolves too."

"Y'all have wolves up in these parts?"

"We didn't used to. Settlers killed them all, but then the government came in; been releasing a few every year. Dan would put those little trackers on them and he'd make sure they weren't being killed or dying off." Then the old man looked around and leaned in conspiratorially. "But between you and me, I don't think they'll find him."

With his curiosity peaked, Jay leaned in as well to speak in hushed tones. "Why's that? They got helicopters out there. Seems like they brought enough force to bear."

"They do, but it won't do them any good. See, the last couple times Dan came in he was real quite; didn't talk much. So last time I seen him, I asked him how he's doing. He said something strange. Said that in all the years he's been here, cougar numbers never changed; never went up, never went down. Then the deer were always just about the same too. The way he tells it, the numbers of predators and prey normally seesaws up and down. More deer, less plants, but less predators. Then the predators have more to eat so they do the birds and the bees and then there's more of them up until there's not enough food and they die off, then it all goes back the other way."

After another quick look around he continued, "Having nothing change, that's just not natural. Then he said he thinks he figured out why, but he needs proof, first, and he can't talk about it. Said he's getting some expert friends of his from the government to come down here, once he finds whatever evidence he's looking for. That's the last I saw of him."

Jay shot him a sly smile and asked, "So what do *you* think he found out there?"

"I think big Dan found something he wasn't supposed to. Some big government secret. Then when he told them, they had to shut him up. He's probably down in Guantanamo, or worse."

"Well thanks very much, sir. I'll watch myself out there."

"Are you one of those logging boys?"

"Yup, startin' tomorrow."

"Well, you seem like a good kid son, here." Pops unlocked a glass case near the window and took out a small pocket knife with a tiger print handle. The top side of the handle was severely bleached by the sun to the point that the orange was yellow and the black was grey. "I've had this damn thing for years now, and no one's so much as glanced at it. The only tool a man needs is a good knife. This is one of those cheap-o, china made, slap jobs. It won't hold an edge, but it'll do you."

Suddenly his mind flashed back to the sharp teeth, wide mouth, and yellow eyes. He squeezed the little knife, validating that it was real before pocketing it. "Thanks, Pops. I'll see you 'round."

"I'd better. Listening is a dying art," he said with a smile and a wave.

The bell above the door chimed and clattered as Jay exited the little shop.

Five: Homesteading

"Josiah Jones?"

Jay opened his eyes, rising out of the shallow nap he had been taking. He had been resting on a bench at the bus station, arms folded, head nodded. Looking up, he saw a black kid with his hair braided in tight cornrows that dangled down just past his shoulders. He couldn't be older than eighteen or twenty. The boy was scrawny and had bags under his expectant eyes. He wore a simple white tank top with sweat stains, along with sturdy, reinforced blue jeans and muddy work boots.

"Um, yeah, that's me. What can I do you for?"

"Ha, third try." The young man grew much more energetic and stuck out his hand. "Name's Zack, uh, Roan. Sir. I guess. I'm your getaway driver. If you got your shit, let's get going. I'm running the mess line tonight and I don't want to get busted up for being late on mealtime."

The kid seemed in high spirits, but nervous. Jay couldn't blame him; talking to people was a skill that had taken him years to feel comfortable with; if you could call it comfortable. Well, like his daddy always said, "Make 'em laugh, and you got 'em."

"You drive *and* cook? Tell me you're loaded and I'll marry you on the spot," he said with a chuckle.

Zack laughed nervously. "Sorry to disappoint, but my skills don't go past haircuts, computers, and driving. Hope you like chili."

With mock disappointment, Jay groaned, "Aww, shucks. I guess you can add breaking hearts to the list." With another good natured chuckle, he picked up his things and looked around. "Well, where're we parked?"

Zack pointed, and Jay's heart soared. Sitting majestically in the parking lot was a brand new, midnight blue, 4-door, lifted, extended bed and extended cab pickup truck that was lifted so high it was almost a monster truck. It was loaded down with saplings that had their root bulbs wrapped up in potato sacks. They stood

31

about as tall as a man, and rested next to big brown sacks labeled "POTATOES". Reuse what you got, he mused.

The beautiful behemoth was covered in liberal splashing's of mud and dirt, with gravel caked into the deep treads. It was the most beautiful thing he'd ever laid eyes on. As they climbed up into the cab Jay marveled at all the features in the dash. He had no idea what most of them did, but it was impressive that there were so many. As he sunk into the heated seats, he breathed a contented sigh and slipped into nirvana.

Zack turned on the ignition, and some flavor of hard-core gangster rap met his ears. Jay was impressed with how the rapper was spitting out verses and could still be understood, even if he was raunchy, egotistical, and self-aggrandizing. At each bass line in the music, the subwoofers in the massive speakers vibrated his entire body. He could feel every note as the bass thrummed through him like a rhythmic earthquake. If he were a betting man, he'd guess that the music could be picked up on a Richter scale. The massive V8 engine roared to life, vibrating him into a whole new universe. He inhaled another deep, long, blissful breath and settled in. Nirvana.

— — — — — — — — — —

The long roads twisted around the mountains like a serpent, coiling up, down, and around the rolling peaks. The sides of the road were thick with trees, so much so that they blocked the spectacular view for most of the journey; but when he was able to get a peek, he enjoyed the picturesque scenes of green valleys and snow peaked mountains. The mountain ranges stretched so far over the land that they faded into blue mountains, that then faded into the blue skies, in turn. A nearly seamless transition between land and sky. The road wove back and forth, and upward so steeply you could see the road right below you. Jay marveled at the sheer stone faces that had been blasted out of the mountain walls to create the roads here. The rough stones were pulled back to reveal their striations and multicolored layers, displaying all their shades of grey and

32

brown. The tall cliffs loomed over the truck, covering them in their shadows and standing like giants over the roadway. Every detail of the land entranced him with its raw natural beauty.

They continued climbing upward and eventually achieved a proper elevation. Jay's ears had been popping the entire drive. They drove through areas that had been clear cut, and there, the view they provided was as breathtaking as it was heart-stopping. Without the trees to his side, Jay realized just how close the road was to the cliff. The line between a secure path and a doomed fall off a mountain was the width of a gnat's ass. Looking into the abyssal drop made him grip the seat like he was a cat at bath time. The enchantment had evaporated a bit, and he was reminded of just how small he was in the face of nature itself, enchanting or not.

The rocky, packed dirt road was just big enough for the truck, and being seated in the passenger seat, Jay got a front row seat to the nearly vertical cliff. It was all too easy to imagine the truck slipping on a loose patch of dirt or rock and tumbling down, down, down an entire mountain; only to lay crumpled at the bottom like a balled up piece of paper; and it did *NOT* help that Zack was driving faster than any sane person would *ever* go on a road like this. To his credit, though, the kid had some laser focus, his eyes locked onto the road ahead of them, his head bobbing opposite of the truck's movements to keep steady. Jay hadn't even realized he had been white-knuckling the door handle.

Zack smiled and stole little glances out Jay's window. "I fucking love the view up here."

Jay chanced a peek out the window, and had to admit, the sight of a squat, lonely mountain with a snow-covered dome rising above a rolling sea of green was breathtaking. Jay imagined what it would have looked like before it erupted. Angelic clouds lazily drifted off in the distance and kissed the mountain's peak. However, the bone shattering drop was equally breathtaking, but for all the wrong reasons. All Jay could manage was a stifled, "Mm hm." He did a quick side glance at the door lock to make sure it was locked.

"Heights not your thing?"

"Nah," he replied in a gruff, strained voice.

33

Zack's lips curled into a grin that smacked of pure mischief. He quickly tugged the wheel to one side and then back again, lurching the vehicle hard. Jay tightened his grip on the door handle and grabbed the seat as he pushed himself down *hard*. Every muscle in his body was tense with the effort of holding himself in place. With wide eyes and pupils the size of dinner plates, Jay stared at the laughing mad man next to him. The little psycho wasn't even wearing a seat belt.

"What the hell are you doing, you lunatic?" Jay roared.

"Chill, bro, just having some fun."

Jay still gripped the inside of the truck for dear life. "Just... keep it on the road." He could hear his heart pounding in his ears.

The road flattened out somewhat and began to go down at a safe, steady angle. As it declined, Jay was able to relax a little.

Zack turned the music down and asked, "So, what kind of a name is 'Josiah Jones', anyway? What, you like a superhero or somethin'?"

The question caught him off guard and he balked, trying to find the right words while recovering from his scare.

"Or are you, like, some kind of hard-boiled detective, tryin' to take down a big gangsta?"

Jay finally caught up with the conversation and cracked a little grin. "Nah, you got it all wrong, I'm a gun slinging lawman, trying to find the bandit's, what burned his wife and shot his farm."

Zack's chuckle quickly turned into a full belly laugh as the joke set in, "You know, you're a'ight." He cranked up the music with a smile and the two continued to make their way down the winding mountain roads; still too quickly for Jay's liking.

—————————

They pulled into camp close to dusk. The sun was part way through its descent and soon it would brush the tops of the trees. Their noble steed came to a halt in a dirt patch, spitting clods of dried mud and gravel from its cyclopean tires. A billowing dust cloud and rocks issued forth from its undercarriage, and choked up the air around them. Zack jumped out, and once he cleared the dust cloud, took a deep breath of mountain air. He let it out slowly with a long sigh. "Home sweet home. Hey, help me get his shit out, these bitches be heavy."

They opened the tailgate of the truck and hauled out the saplings. They each grabbed one and began rolling them on their base toward a row of other saplings that had already been delivered. The tree itself wasn't terribly heavy, but the root base and the dirt were like lead weights. After an exhausting few minutes they managed to lug the last tree over.

Zack set it into place with a grunt of exertion. "I'll tell you, I can't wait to get done with mess so I can get back to Beat Down. I've been thinkin' about it all day, and I think I gots a strat to deal with the third stage attack."

Jay looked at him with a bemused look. "Boy, I have absolutely *no* idea what the hell you just said to me."

"Oh, uh, I've got this video game called Beat Down, it's all music themed fighting game, and you got to pay attention to the beat to avoid the attacks. I'm stuck on this one hoe. She's this DJ boss. When her health gets down low she hits you with this sucker shot called Turn Table and it *fucks* your health bar."

Jay just stared at him with a wall-eyed expression, unsure how to respond.

"Ah, nevermind. Most of the guys here don't play either. Where I grew up, you was either into gangs, or you was into games, and I di'n have enough friends for hoops. I kinda go down my own rabbit hole sometimes, you know? Get lost up in my own head. Honestly, if Mat wasn't such a chill guy I'd have blown this place. Pigs won't let me have any computers or anything because I gotta charge, cybercrimes and some bullshit, so I aint supposed to be on the internet. But since there ain't no wifi in the fucking woods, he lets me have a little somethin', somethin'."

"Ah, yeah, they had some video games in the common room. They were never my speed. I don't have the hand eye coordination for that kind of thing."

While they began to unload the sacks of potatoes, Zack asked, "What did they have?"

"Somethin' where I was a soldier. Metal of Duty? I don't remember the name. Everyone else was flyin' 'round like hamsters on coffee. I was happy when I could keep from walkin' into a wall. Plus it hurt my head if I looked at it for too long."

"Ah yeah, yeah that one's for twitch gamer freaks that chug Gamer Gas all night, then have a heart attack at twenty-two."

Jay set his sack of potatoes down with the others and gave an absurd laugh, "What in the Sam hell is 'Gamer Gas'?"

"Sugar water. It makes your blood thick and gives you a heart attack if you drink too much; I'm not even half joking. I'm more of ah, a *green* gamer, you feel? The day they made that shit legal was the happiest damn day of my life. No foolin', literally on my birthday. I had to get my big bro to buy it for me 'cause I wasn't legal, but still. Smoke, game, chill. Best fucking birthday present of my life."

"Well," Jay said, hefting the last of the sacks into place, "if I ever want to switch my brain off after a long hard day, and fumble around and watch some pretty lights, I'll let you know."

Zack visibly perked up at that. "Hell yeah, man. Honestly, you play better high. You think less and you just play. Y'know? You don't, like, overanalyze and shit."

With a skyward stretch and a long groan, Jay popped his back so loud that he could feel it down to his toes. He surveyed the camp, looking for where he could bed down. The camp was fairly straight forward, and was well organized from what he could see. There was a motor pool of machinery and work vehicles, but he wasn't interested in them at the moment. Continuing his search, he spied a row of about a dozen school busses, all lined up next to each other. Their whole paint job inspired the impression of a log cabin on wheels. Each one was painted a matt brown with darker brown stripes painted along them horizontally. Light brown circles painted on the ends really helped to sell the illusion. He motioned to them and asked, "Those the bunk houses?"

Zack nodded and said, "Yup, I'll show you ours."

As they walked up the row of busses, Jay suspected they were painted brown for another reason; to help hide all the mud and dirt. The log cabin paint job probably helped make them feel homier, too. Taking a peek through the backdoor windows, he was able to see inside and appreciate the effort put into making them comfortable. Each one had major renovations done to it. The insides had been gutted and all the seats removed. Beds had been installed, along with cabinets above and below the beds. It was a clever use of space. The front of the buses had some furniture installed just behind the driver's seat to make it feel like a little living room.

Solar panels were mounted onto the roofs so each one had electricity. Some forward thinkers had the foresight to leave the emergency exit untouched, save for the handles being repainted yellow instead of red and the installation of a lock for the inside. The front doors had been modified to open from the outside with a handle, and a bar on the inside could lock them closed. Near each entrance was a little numbered metal plate that slid into a groove. Each slate was numbered, and reminded him of house addresses.

Zack stopped at the very last one. "This is us, number sixty-three."

"Sixty-three," Jay echoed. He looked around, confused. "I ain't the best with numbers, but there looks to be a few less than sixty-three busses."

"Yeah, Mat's got a few other operations like this, but he oversees this one personally. He's got other guys running the other jobs. He's been teaching me the business part of it all; thinkin' I might move up somewhere someday. Brother's got good hustle. No clear cutting. He leaves some of the old growth, 'cause shade and shit helps the little ones grow, and it stops mudslides; plus he replants. All that stuff he does really plays the system, too. Gets tax breaks and shit left and right. Then 'cause he keeps costs down, he can bump up wages. Same work, mo' money. And trust me, cash helps keep the nastier people in line; usually."

"Couple of bad apples 'round here?"

Zack just laughed and showed him inside. "One or two I guess, but mostly just the one. The guy's he hires are all on the same beat, and most come straight out of lockup, so we all get it, you know? Everybody's just looking to jumpstart their lives, and this place is nice. You get a good work record working here that ain't *the record*, so then you can go other places after a while and not stay some street thug to employers, you feel? A second chance. So, uh, the bed on the left end is yours. I gotta get to mess and get grub started. Catch you later, dude."

Zack made his exit, and Jay shuffled over to his bed. He stuffed his pack into one of the cupboards and sat. It wasn't the Ritz, but it was comfortable, and way better than what he had been expecting. He lay down and breathed a sigh of relief at the end of his long journey. Suddenly realizing how tired he'd become, he shut his weary eyes and immediately fell asleep, shoes on and all.

* * * * * * * * *

It was dark. The Night Sun was gone and the Twinkling Lights were littered in the Above. It took tentative steps through the forest as it passed over ferns, logs and other debris. It liked being out at night. It could see well in the dark. It could see even better with the Night Sun. Despite its absence tonight, It could still see perfectly, but It had to move slowly. Slower than usual. It wanted to bolt, to run, to chase, but It would scare the prey. It tested the air, sniffing.

The unmistakable scent of Claw Paw filled its nostrils. The Claw Paw had entered its territory one and one and one days ago. Now it was getting close. The Claw Paw had marked a tree. It was fresh. It sniffed the air again. There was something new on the wind. Horned Food. The Claw Paw was on a hunt of its own, it seemed. It hated competition. All meat belonged to It. Competition had to be made into meat. With nostrils flared, It followed the scent of the intruder.

While It quietly stalked through the night It had time to think. It had been eating well recently. It had been a very long time since It had tasted Tall One meat; since before the Black Snow. It had forgotten how tasty they were. These new packs of Tall Ones though, they were different from the old ones. They changed the forest, the land, the mountains. It tried to avoid Tall Ones, for they were bizarre creatures, and could pack hunt, but sometimes It would find one alone, separated, and vulnerable; like the last one.

A fond memory wafted through Its thoughts. It remembered back during the Snow Land times, It could sneak into their territory when the Night Sun was dim and could take their young; sometimes one and one in a single night without ever being seen. The young dripped with sweet, succulent fat. These new tall ones were like their cubs. More fat, more flavor. And the prey beasts they took into their Wood Caves were fat too. Small, trapped, alone. Thinking about Its recent successes caused a long line of saliva to drip from Its mouth.

It sniffed again. Good smell. Meat. The Claw Paw had taken its kill. Focusing Its hearing It could pick up the sound of the competition gorging itself in the distance. It crept closer, taking Its time with each step so as not to alert the prey. Slowly, methodically, It approached with the skilled silence of a true and seasoned killer. The last thing the Claw Paw ever saw was a glowing disk of yellow light, rhythmically pulsing in the dark forest.

Six: Work Hard, Heal Hard

The holy scent of food elegantly drifted over Jay's nostrils and roused him from his sleep. With a dull clunk, he heard a bowl being set on the small drawers by his bed. Jay sat up and found it was dark out, but by the very faint blue tint to the shadows outside, he guessed it was early morning.

"Morning, sleeping beauty," came a scratchy, crackling voice, "thought a little room service might help get you out of bed for your first day. Don't get used to it."

Jay became all too aware of how hungry he was as he wiped away the drool from the corner of his mouth. He grabbed the bowl and took a brief moment to appreciate it. It had a thick broth, almost like chili. Each spoonful was loaded with hearty chunks of soft potato, carrots, celery, and just enough kick of pepper to warm his blood from the morning chill. Only once he spooned every last bit of slow cooked goodness from the bowl did he slow down to breathe. With a long, satisfied moan he begrudgingly stood up and stepped outside, bowl in hand.

After a night's rest and a belly full of food he took stock of the camp in more detail. The whole camp was basically a large circle that had been gouged out of the forest. The stumps had been removed, the trees taken away and for the most part the area was flat. There were logging trucks parked, ready to haul off the processed trees. There was also a mix of machinery that he couldn't quite figure out, but it was impressive, nonetheless. He was, however, able to identify an impressively sized backhoe. At least he knew *one* of them by name. Around one of the workstations, there was an assortment of tools that ran the gamut from dirt caked shovels and old axes with recently sharpened blades, to chainsaws with smudges of grease painted over their bodies, piles of carefully wound ropes and safety equipment, hard hat, and cross-saws. There were crowbars and a dozen other tools all around in an organized mess. They were all stored in and around a wooden shed, along with another machine he didn't recognize. Maybe an angle grinder for sharpening chainsaw teeth. Finally, he found what he was looking for. Soft, yellow lights around some tables surrounded a big red school bus. The sounds of clinking dishes, the smell of food and the sound of voices talking and laughing emanated from them.

The red bus buzzed with fluorescent lighting and was remodeled to act like a food truck. It was open on both sides to serve more people and the back of the bus had been renovated into a kitchen. The bus was surrounded by metal, foldable picnic tables. At least there were enough seats for everyone. He always hated going to mess. It was always too open, and more than once someone got shanked mid meal. His mind flashed with the last guy he remembered getting hit like that. The guy who got him knew what he was doing, too. Got him at three sweet spots and twisted the knife so he couldn't be closed up as easily. Jay was pretty sure that guy didn't make it.

He shook his head, shaking off the haunting memories. This was a new place and it seemed more inviting; nice, even. Jay walked over to the open metal shutters and its serving window. A younger Latino man with long, black hair and several tattoos up his arms broke off his conversation as Jay approached and greeted him with an up nod.

The man spoke clear English, but with a thick Mexican accent. "Sup, homes. Whatchu need?"

"Just bringin' this back for you," Jay replied, indicating the bowl.

The man's face lit up as he clapped loudly and took the bowl. "Ah, shit. Gracias, amigo. Most of these *cerdos* just leave their shit out there, and whoever's on mess has to clean it up." He then shook the bowl for punctuation. "Hey, you're the new guy, right? Names' Alejandro Garcia," he said, reaching down from the truck to shake hands.

It was a firm shake, but he didn't try to crush Jay's hand. Good kid. "Jay Jones. Pleasure to meet you."

With an indignant snort Alejandro looked around, then back to Jay. "Whatever, man," he said before he tapped the man serving the other window, a slim, young-ish black man in a du rag. "This here's Black George, Mexi George is back in the kitchen with Dorje. You'll probably see them out there today."

"Well if'n you get the chance, thank 'em for the meal. Best damn thing I've had'n a long time."

Alejandro smiled and gave him another up nod. "Aye, gracias amigo." He then turned and shouted into the kitchen, "Oi, ese, you got bumped on that bomb-ass stew, bro."

An excited shout came from the back of the kitchen.

Then off to the side someone shouted from the tables, "Jay!"

He turned toward the shouting and saw Zack waving furiously at him and pointing at an empty seat. Jay chuckled, "I guess I've got a young gentleman caller. It was good meetin' you, Mr. Garcia."

Alejandro leaned out the window and called out, "Hey, man, you too. Careful out there, I don't need someone who cleans up getting his head crushed on day one."

Jay pulled up a seat at the table. Sitting with them was a man he didn't recognize, but as the man greeted him, he remembered his gravelly voice from earlier. He was an older white man, maybe late fifties, but his tan, weathered skin spoke of a life hard lived and made him look much older. He had a military crew cut on the back and sides, but he had clearly let the top go since it looked more like a mop than hair. His hair was a mixture of greys and whites, and if the man wasn't so clean shaven he'd guess the beard was the same way.

"Nice to see you up," came his craggy voice.

The man offered his hand. Jay took it and instantly regretted it. It was like gripping a palm made of wrought iron. The man had a grip that could crush coal into diamonds. Jay winced inwardly and squeezed back, hard, trying to relieve some of the stress.

The man then smiled up at him and said, "Strong handshake. Good kid. Name's Timothy, or Tim if you like."

43

Jay rubbed his tender hand. "What've you got for a hand, hydraulics?"

Tim threw his head back in laughter. "Mechanics hands. You know how it is."

The third man stood up and leaned over the table, extending his hand. He was a middle aged Latino fellow. He had a bald head, shaved smooth, with some salt and pepper stubble coming in. The man was fairly stalky with a gut that protruded far past his waistline, but under the fat Jay could easily see dense muscles tensing and rippling with every little movement.

English was clearly the man's first language but there was a hint of an accent; Jay guessed he was probably second or third generation American. "Hi, there. I'm Earl. I'd love to stay and chat, but I've got to get going. I've got a tree to shimmy up."

Zack grinned mischievously as he said, "I thought you were going in for thirds, big man."

"Screw you, Skinny," he said with a smirk, "not all of us can eat like a dump truck and stay a little boy. Some of us grew up to be big, strong men."

As he walked away Jay couldn't help but notice the truly ridiculous size of the man's calves pulling his pant legs tight around them. With each step the muscles underneath flexed with exaggerated definition. Slowly shaking his head in disbelief he turned back to the table as Tim spoke up.

"Well, newbie, normally you'd be in Mat's trailer all day going over paperwork and such, but he said you've gone over it already, so we'll get right to the hands-on training."

"Speakin' of, where *is* Mat? I ain't seen hide nor hair of him."

Zack chimed in and said, "Brother's in town. Went in this morning, said he was gonna volunteer with the search, talk some stuff over with the sheriff; basically say, 'Aey, none of my boys did it'."

Jay gave him a side eye. "Why come you know so much 'bout the going's on of this place?"

"I told you, I'm training for management, I'mma be big cheese one day," he said, popping the front of his shirt to exaggerate the point.

Jay looked at him incredulously.

At his gaze, Zack's ego visually deflated a bit. "Don't give me that face. Dude, I crunch numbers and logistics for *fun*. Games ain't just about mashing buttons. I like making shit run smooth, streamlined; *sexy*."

"Alright, wise ass, when's he due back?"

"Tonight, I'm picking him up with some more trees. I get to drive the *big* truck."

Jay looked at him quizzically as he remembered how big that magnificent blue stallion he'd rode in on had been. If the pickup wasn't the big one, then, "Which one's the 'big' truck?"

With a hungry look in his eye, Zack pointed toward a massive eighteen-wheeler, already loaded with a full haul of lumber.

Tim eyed them both and grumbled, "If you two love birds are done chit chatting, we've got work to do. Jay, you're with me. All those papers are some good advice, but you've got to see what you're working with. Today's just going to be about how not to get killed, cause trust me, you've got options. Let's go."

Zack left his bowl as the three stood up to walk away. Jay motioned to it and said, "Hey Mister Manager, you'll make happy workers if you make less work."

Zack rolled his eyes and bussed his bowl before running off to get ready.

Tim pointed to another renovated school bus that had been painted blue. This one had no windows and had been reinforced. In front of it were several basic shower stalls on a platform. Shower heads protruded from the side of the bus and over the stalls. "The showers over that way. They're on a three-minute timer so lather up, get the crevices and get out. I'll get you the uniform, I can eyeball your size. Now get going, we're late."

Jay looked at his phone's clock and was astonished at how early it was, he'd also have to charge it soon. "What time do things start around here?"

"We're in the field at oh seven hundred. Takes close to thirty to get there and set up."

"We've got an hour, easy."

Tim gave him a hard look, "Exactly, we're late. Now get moving."

— — — — — — — — — —

The sun was out and Jay was enjoying the beautiful day. Everyone else was complaining about the heat, but the Texan just smiled and let the sweat roll off like it was nothing. How could anyone complain with all this green? Besides, it wasn't *that* hot. When lunch time rolled around, he sat on a log and thought while he chowed down. The day was going by quickly and he was doing his best to remember everything he'd learned, but for now he took a moment to appreciate his surroundings.

This place was nothing like the forests he grew up around. This place was primal. Back home he could walk in the woods, and sure, there were trees and there were bushes, or swamps, or tall grass, but he could still see. Not here. The foliage was so thick and dense from the forest floor to the shrub layer, only small animals could scurry beneath. The shrubbery was like wooded arms with branch-like hands that tangled, twisted, and interlocked to build impenetrable barriers so tight that they blocked light itself. The higher up in the canopy, the stronger the light was able to break through, but not by much. There was no breeze breaking through the branches. The top canopy of the trees were so high it almost gave him a headache to keep looking up. Cutting through the shrubbery to carve a new road for their equipment would be more like mining than lumber work.

The team tunneled deeper, making new roads to bring larger vehicles in and haul lumber out. They would make small offshoots and thin the forest in parts, taking the quality trees that met a certain standard and left the others standing.

He remembered his daddy telling him about the jungle overseas, how oppressive it was, how the trees grew up real tall and pushed down on you with their branches. How you couldn't see more than ten feet in any direction and that was if you were lucky. There were tigers in those jungles; people, too, but what spooked him most were the tigers. Man eaters. Once they got a taste for humans during the war, that was all they craved. Since so many soldiers on both sides were out in small groups, people were back on the menu. Jay was glad there weren't any here. Cougars, sure, but they mostly stayed away from the noise of civilization. He'd never actually seen a cougar in person, but everyone who talked about them said they could easily take down a man. They would stalk their prey for miles. Just out of sight, silent and deadly. They nearly always strike from behind or above.

But this wasn't the time for daydreaming. Jay shook his head and pulled his mind out of the clouds. He ran over everything he had learned as he watched and ate. The Fallers worked with chain saws to fell the trees. The Buckers worked with the Fallers to trim the tops and branches off before sectioning it to the right size. Then if a tree had dangerous snag branches that could fall off, then the Tree Climbers come in. Those big, crazy SOB's would go up with giant chainsaws and do all the topping and branch removal before the Faller got in to bring it down.

Then there was the harvester. It was truly an intimidating piece of machinery. A metal framed, glass cabin sat atop a pair of wide, sturdy treads. From the back of the mobile platform came a long, hydraulic powered scorpion tail that bent over the front, but in lieu of a stinger it had a metal hand the size of a truck cab. The mechanical hand came equipped with a buzz saw and rotors built into the palm to slide trees through and cut them down. That one machine did the work of all three other jobs in one go. The only problem was it was too big to fit certain places, so it stayed on the main paths. Jay looked up at the cozy little cab of the harvester. One of the biggest men he'd ever seen sat contentedly in the air conditioned unit while he waited for the rest of the team to make room enough for him to come in and do his job. Jay didn't know what his job *was* exactly, the man had just sat in there all day.

As he wondered, Tim called out and got Jay's attention, "Ten's up, newbie, let's go."

Jay shoveled the last of his sandwich into his mouth and choked it down as he jogged over to his new lesson. The lesson which was, funnily enough, called Choke Setting. He watched as Alejandro, Black George and two men, who he guessed were the other George and Dorje, fastened huge chains and hooks to the lumber to secure it. The lesson was quick and simple enough to understand.

While they worked, Tim cracked a smile and leaned toward Jay. "Look real close at what Dorje's doing. He's hands down the best at this." Then, louder, he called out, "This guy's tough as nails, ain't that right, Dorje?"

Dorje was a wiry, tan, older Asian man. His round features suggested Chinese, maybe, but there were subtleties that made Jay think he was Vietnamese, maybe Laotian. He put out a hand and said, "Howdy, friend. I've never met anyone named Dorje before. Where are you from, if you don't mind me asking?"

Dorje shook his hand and chuckled warmly. "It is good to meet you, friend. I am from Tibet." He chuckled again and returned to his work. He spoke slowly, each word heavily accented. "And yes, I very best. I do this work back home, before I come here. You want to hear?"

With a polite nod, Jay said, "Sure."

Dorje hoisted up a chain, set it in place then leaned against the log to rest.

"I moved to Vietnam after the French, but before the Americans, to be with my wife, and when the war ended the Americans left. We had to flee Ho Chi Minh or we be getting killed.

48

We go to the helicopters, they say 'no room'! We go to the boats, they say 'no room'! My father was fisherman. I had his little fishing boat. So I took my family, my friends, and anyone who could fit. We tried to escape to Taiwan. We had twenty-five people in twenty-foot boat. For two weeks, we in ocean. Then, we had no food and no water; drifting for three whole days. Oil drilling platform, they see us and take us in. The next day there is big storm. Very lucky. But here, we don't wait for lucky. We make for safety, safety, safety!"

Tim let out a warm, amused chuckle. "That's right. Safety, safety, safety." With the lesson concluded, Dorje and his team got back to work, and Tim led him to the next station. Suddenly, out from the crystal clear sky, came an almighty crack, like raging thunder. It echoed long through the trees, and he could feel the sound on his skin. Jay was so startled by the noise he nearly leapt out of his skin, flying straight up like a startled cat. He wheeled around just in time to see a humongous branch slam into the ground with a powerful thud. Looking way up into the tree, Jay saw Earl strapped in around the top branches and wielding a five-foot chainsaw. Earl spotted him and waved before continuing his work.

Tim laughed at him and gave him a hearty slap on the back. "Come on, newbie. Don't need you having a heart attack in the field." As they walked over to the next station, the sound of a chainsaw roared behind them.

They met up with Zack who was marking some measurements on several stripped timbers. "Sup, guys? Come to learn the good shit about log grading and scaling?"

Just then the sound of the parked harvester with the scorpion tail roared to life.

Tim's scratchy voice strained to shout over the behemoth engine. "**Just a quick rundown so he knows all the parts of the operation, not a ton of safety to go over with this one.**"

Zack nodded and turned to Jay, stepping closer to be heard and gesturing while he talked. "**So all I do here is measure these things to make sure they're all good. Right size and thickness, all that. I look 'em up and down to make sure the quality checks out. I** also decide which timber becomes building wood and which turns into pulpwood."

"The hell is pulpwood?" Jay shouted back.

"It's the crap wood that-"

At that moment the harvester drowned out his words by clamping onto a thick, towering tree with its massive claws. It extended its spinning blade into the trunk and lifted the entire tree from its severed base. The rotors clamped on, pushing the tree through the palm of the metal hand, forcefully ripping off limbs and strips of bark. It turned the tree sideways and cut off a measured length of the trunk. Then it shoved more of the tree through until it was the same length as the first segment. It cut off the second section to fall with the first, and repeated the process until the whole tree was stripped and cut. The whole thing took less than a minute.

The monster rolled forward and grabbed another tree to continue with its brutal efficiency. It cut and lifted the timber, same as the first, but this time the stump end of the tree was facing toward the group; and the machine was far too close. Jay looked up, and with the reflexes of a cat, he grabbed Zack's collar and threw them both to the ground. Tim saw it coming, the same time Jay, and had hit the dirt with them. The severed tree was gripped by the rotors and launched like a one ton piston straight through the space Zack's head had been.

Tim leapt to his feet and flew into a rage. He jumped up to the cab of the harvester and banged so hard on the glass Jay thought he'd put his fist through it. "Mclean," he screamed, "what kind of shit are you trying to pull, you ass backward, inbred, degenerate!"

The man inside opened the door, stooped through the porthole and towered over Tim. Tim stood his ground and wasn't fazed in the least by the intimidating figure before him. Mclean was a white guy, but he had built up a healthy tan. The man was practically a giant, looming over six and a half feet tall. The sides of his head were shaved and the top had two thick, black braids that were draped down to the back of his neck. The bridge of his nose

50

was thick and crooked, having clearly been broken in his past; probably many times. His eyes were just a touch too wide set and his ears stuck straight out to the side. On his chin, he sported a thick goatee that joined up with his short mustache.

Peeking out from under the sleeve of his T-shirt, Jay noticed the tail end of a flaming, orange tattoo. Down the man's other arm was a long, deep scar that ran its length down to his wrist. On top of it all, the man had a classic rooster build. Jay had seen it often in the yard. Guy's would lift too much, but completely neglect their legs; not that there was much room to run in prison. His whole build made him look like a boulder on stilts. The man hopped down and landed on both feet, but Jay noted that as he stepped, he favored one side over the other.

The entire time Tim hadn't relented. "We've gone almost a full year without some career ending injury and then you almost pop Skinny's head like a damn grape. And you, especially you, should take the two damn seconds to check what the hell's going on around them. So you had better have the best damn reason in the fucking world why you can't open those fat little eyes of yours, and do *not* keep me waiting."

Mclean was turning redder by the second. His jaw was clenched and Jay would have sworn he was about to grind his own teeth into dust. Mclean was so red faced it looked like his head might have exploded from the pressure. At the end of Tim's tirade the dam broke. His voice was booming and could be heard over all the power tools and equipment as he roared, "And what was that little shit stain doing near my goddamn equipment? You think I can fucking see *everything* in this baby? Like I'm supposed to just know when some retard wanders around with a fucking death wish?"

"Yes! It's your fucking job!"

It was subtle, but there was a slight limp to his step as Mclean stepped closer to Tim in their shouting match.

Tim didn't give an inch while Mclean continued to roar, "Well then why don't you keep that blind bitch on a damn leash, far the fuck from me, 'cause if he gets in my way again I'll crack that little faggot's neck like the chicken he is!"

51

Tim was loading up his next volley of insults, but half way through the thought he visibly relaxed as he seemed to enter a kind of anger nirvana. In a voice that sounded like rocks in a blender, and was as cool as ice, he growled, "If you so much as breathe on him I'll finish what that chainsaw started."

The threat made the bigger man balk as he subconsciously touched the long scar running up his arm. "Just keep that little freak out of my way."

With that he crawled back into the cabin and began furiously ripping apart trees.

Zack was staring scorch marks into the ground and shaking as Tim stalked back over, knuckles clenched so tightly he probably *could* crush coal into diamonds. Though as he approached his demeanor visibly softened. He put a hand on Zack who flinched away a little.

"Right," Tim said as he took his hand back, "how are you holding up, Skinny?"

Even though his face was downcast, Jay could see a tear or two fall from the young man.

Tim grumbled, "Ok, we're done for today."

The three of them hiked back to camp slowly, letting Zack set the pace as they walked on either side of him. It took a while, but as the sun beamed down upon them, the walk down the dirt road was nice in its own way. They returned to camp and stepped into their bus. No one spoke a word the whole time.

Jay hadn't taken the time to really explore his new home at all. It was very comfortable, considering it was just a renovated school bus. There were four chairs that were scattered around, and a small table with some playing cards spread around. The floor had a tough carpet, but it was the industrial kind that offices used, so it was cheap and easy to clean. There was no fridge, probably to keep animals from breaking in, but there was a little T.V built into the wall in front of a large bean bag, which they let Zack slide onto. He slumped back and stared at the black screen, despondently. Tim tapped Jay and nodded outside.

"It's not my place to talk about it, but he's not ok right now. Sometimes home isn't home, and I don't think that kid ever had one to begin with. I don't want that shit sack coming around, so I'm going to head out and get Mat. Since you're not trained yet, it's your job to just sit here with him until I get back. Can you do that?"

Jay nodded. "Yes'sir."

Tim just shook his head at the world. "I'll be back by twenty one hundred."

With that, he walked off toward the truck, still shaking his head in disbelief. Jay stood alone, not entirely sure what to do with himself. He loitered for several moments before looking up into the sky. The clouds were painted across the entire horizon as if they were painted by a renaissance master. Large, white mounds of fluff shone brilliantly in the sunlight. They were contrasted here and there by darker clouds that threatened rain, but would hold their peace for now. The only word he could think to describe it was "heavenly".

He closed his eyes tight and fought back a tear. Had anything really changed for him? Even here, surrounded by all this beauty, without a wall or fence for a hundred miles, right here in this moment, he still felt trapped. Trapped with predators. All he could do was take a page from Tim's book and shake his head at the world before he went inside.

Zack was still staring into the abyss, tear marks down his cheeks. Looking around the cabin, Jay saw that someone had plastered a giant pot leaf sticker on one of the cabinets. He guessed that that one belonged to Zack, and could assume its contents. Inside he retrieved a small, psychedelically colored glass pipe. The glass had been shaped to resemble a little frog, and along with the pipe he collected a baggy of weed and a box of matches. Pulling one of the seats over to the bean bag, he sat down and held the items in his hands for several moments before asking, "Ok, I was always a beer man, how in the sam hell do I use one of these?"

Zack halfheartedly turned his head and silently took the pipe and baggy. His voice was little more than a mumble as he opened the baggy, "First you got to load your bowl. You don't want to over pack it or else it won't light." He put some of what looked like a ball of moss into the opening on the back of the frog. The powerful aroma of the weed was a surprisingly pleasant mixture of mint and lemon with a dash of skunk. It was nearly overpowering in the enclosed space, but it was kind of nice, sort of; in its own way. Zack shook the box of matches and drew one out. "Then you light a stick, let the cush catch a little and then toke. You'll want to cough, but just hold it. You wanna use wood matches so you don't get all that gasoline chemical shit from lighters."

Jay was handed the loaded pipe and awkwardly tried to hold it while he lit a match. It began to slowly smolder, so he held it up to his lips and inhaled deeply. The smoke hit him hard and it caused him to splutter, half coughing and half choking, but held it in. He counted slowly in his head and got to seven before smoke erupted out of him like a dragon. Coughing and spluttering he doubled over, a long strand of drool making its way closer to the floor with every lung clenching hack.

A little, mischievous grin crept its way onto Zack's face as he tried not to smile. The cocky little bastard took the pipe, skillfully lit a match one handed and took the biggest rip he could, sucking air in for several seconds and holding it, the entire time giving Jay a sneaky little side eye.

Jay felt like he was going to cough up a lung, and there was Zack, taking his time and blowing lazy smoke rings into the air. Jay gave another hard, bronchial cough and said, "Here I am," he was able to choke out between fits, "dyin' over here, coughin' myself to death and yer just over there makin' shapes."

Zack finally let out his first choked cough and let himself slump into the bag. His head rolled back and he just let his limbs hang. He closed his eyes and they simply sat there for a time. Eventually Zack cleared his throat and mumbled, "I'm sorry you have to be here, dude."

Jay felt a tingling in his lips and sat there making smacking sounds before he answered, "Eh, it ain't nothin'. Hell, the way I figure it, I get a day's vacation. A day-cation. I should go an' make that a word."

Zack chuckled. "Congratulations, you just had your first high-dea."

Several moments went by in silence. After a while Zack turned his limp head to look over at Jay and asked, "Tim tell you anything?"

Jay was sitting there zoned out and making little pinching motions with his hands. He didn't respond immediately, his brain processing the fact that a question had been asked. His response was unfocused and lazy. "Nnnnno. He di'nt."

Zack returned to looking at the ceiling. "Yeah, I guess he wouldn't. He's a good guy, but I guess you are too. You're a good guy Jay." They sat there for a little while before Zack picked the conversation back up. "You know how I said it was games or gangs where I'm from?"

Jay was slowly waving to himself in the reflection of the television, thoroughly entertained by his doppelganger. "Uh huh."

"Well, the other reason I chose games was my step dad was a banger. He was slingin' drugs, cooking, growing, selling guns. I think the only thing he didn't do was pimp, but, I don't know. He used to get high and beat the shit out of my mom. Then I got old enough and stood up to him a little, then he'd beat the shit out of me too. Did I tell you what I was put in for?"

Jay turned and looked up, thinking. "Nnnnnno."

"I made some friends online, they'd hack shit. Nothing big, online profiles, break into people's game libraries, shit like that. Well one night I left my mic on, they heard what's going on in the background. They say that shit ain't cool, so they show me some stuff. About a week later my stepdad's going down for identity theft and child porn. He'd been texting with a high schooler he was dealing to, and that was how she paid. Then just to really fuck him up I pinged some IP addresses south of the boarder and talked to him about buying guns on a throwaway. Made it look like he was doing some terrorist shit. Well, I kind of got high on the power and kept hacking stuff."

Jay gave him a look and raised an eyebrow.

Zack caught the stare and quickly back peddled. "No, no, I didn't frame nobody else. I just hacked stuff. What got me was trying to get onto a government server that turned out to be a sting. So, no computer for a while. Then sometimes if people start yelling at me, it's like, it's like I'm a little kid again, you know? And I can't-" he began tearing up and stopped talking.

Jay leaned far out of his chair, nearly falling out, and nudged Zack in the arm. "Hey, I know what you mean about goin' back to places you left. What I do, is when I catch myself doin' that, is I look around and ask myself, 'Do I like where I am now? Is it better than where I was?' If even a'one of those answers is 'no', than I try and change it. If they're yes, than I focus on what's good around me. Hell, just a few days ago I was sharing a room with cockroaches and fleas, and I was thinkin' 'bout doin' sommit' real stupid to get out of there; then Mat gave me an'different option. So keep your options open, is the point I'm trying to make, I think. I'm sorry, I'm starting to feel it real strong."

They shared a quiet laugh and leaned back in their chairs, passing the pipe back and forth. The world became a little bit crisper around the edges, and colors were more interesting than they had been before. He noticed little details he never would have found himself thinking about, pondering the size of various objects around him. Content that it was very much working, he grabbed a plastic controller from near the television. "Ok, show me this boss you're stuck on."

Seven: Missing Persons

It was getting dark out and Jay could hear everyone getting back, putting equipment away, running the showers, heading to mess; the simple sounds of tired men after a long day. Zack was already asleep in bed. Jay was deeply pondering the color orange on the handle of his pocket knife when he heard a truck pulling into camp. He stepped outside and heard a door slam. Tim blew past him and stomped into the bus. He only mumbled a curt, "Night," before he violently kicked off his boots and went to bed.

He saw Mat walking around, chatting briefly here and there with some of the other workers before going into his trailer. It was a little camper with a tow hitch, the kind a single man might take on a short vacation. Jay followed and knocked on the door.

"It's open."

Inside, Mat was sitting at a table surrounded by papers and rummaging through a cardboard box. There were filing cabinets filling most of the space and a little bed in the back with a curtain in front of it. Mat's face was tired and his eyes said more than words ever could as to the fatigue and how disheartened he felt.

Jay leaned against the wall and gave him a knowing look. "That bad, huh?"

"You were there, from what I hear. You should know."

Jay sat down across from Mat while he fished out a bottle of rum from a box. He held up two glasses, but Jay waved him off. "Bad memories."

"Fair enough."

"I'm guessin' Tim di'n take it well?"

Mat poured himself a shot and slammed it back. "Not at all. Without getting into the nitty gritty, all I can do at the moment is document what happened and not renew any contracts. Mclean owns that harvester and we're locked in, short of him actually injuring someone. And before you say anything, no, I did not sign

57

that contract. Turns out one of my, now ex managers, at another site runs in the same circles as him. Really put me in a bad spot. Fucking nepotism."

"Well since you di'n sign anything, what's the problem?"

Mat slammed back another shot and poured himself a third. "The problem is, the guy had authority to hire outside help, which puts us here now. Trust me, I've had lawyers look it over and each one tells me the same thing."

Jay let out a long breath and slumped into his seat. "Well, change of topic. How'd the search for that missing fella go?"

"Dan Harving? Went just as well as anything else today," he said, sipping on the little glass.

Jay gave him an inquisitive look, but wasn't sure what to ask.

Mat took another sip and put the glass down, looking into it like how a man stares into fire. "We found... some things."

His friend just sat, patiently, letting him find the words.

"It wasn't a robbery. His pack was found, his side arm, his rifle, a pile of ammo just lying there. If it was some crazy hill person they'd have taken his things; at least the guns. We found his pants. No damage to them, they were just lying there. His boots were gone along with his shirt and coat. The pants, it looked like someone picked him up and they just fell off him, straight down." Mat drained the glass and stared up at the ceiling, clearly distressed, but still searching for a handle on his own thoughts. "We found his teeth, Jay."

It was at that, he felt his blood run cold, his heart sink, and his stomach drop. "Teeth?"

It took a few moments, but Mat found his voice again. "Just a few, and there was a little blood on them. And the dogs, man. Trained tracking dogs refused, fucking *refused,* to pick up the scent. The handlers had never seen anything like it. Dogs roll in dead critters. Dogs *live* to chase things. Each one they brought in would get the scent, follow it to the same spot and stop; just stop. Or run. Or cry."

Jay was at a loss for words. He was no expert hunter. The biggest thing he ever hunted were pollywogs in the streams as a kid, but there wasn't a damn thing in this world he could think of that would make a dog stop a hunt.

"That's not all. So, when a person dies out there, all manner of critters go to eat them and they just eat through the clothes. They checked the, oh what'd they call it, the scat; the animal shit in the area. No cloth in any of it. They said that the little bones like on the fingers will get eaten and then shit out too, but there weren't any bones either. I don't know what happened to that man, but it gives me the creeps. Tomorrow I'm going to have a talk with everyone, basic safety stuff while out in the field. Maybe implement a buddy system if anyone goes out too far from the main site."

"Yup, I'd reckon that's a good plan. Shit, you're almost makin' me reconsider that drink."

"Ha. Well then, change of topic, besides the unpleasantness, how'd your first day go?"

* * * * * * * * *

It was dark. The Night Sun had begun to open its eye, but only a sliver. Soon the eye would open and the night would be like day. Good time to hunt when the eye was open. That was when the prey walked in the cool night air.

For now, though, It would enjoy its meal. As It traveled towards Its hidden treasure, It fondly remembered the night before when It had eaten the best parts of the Claw Paw. It had started with the special parts in the body. It relished the tough, chewy meat lump in the chest. It delighted while it devoured the long flat piece that looked like a stone. It savored the feeling of slurping down each of the two chest sacks in turn. It saved the eyes for last. It loved the feeling as its teeth sliced into the squishy, yet tough meat.

59

With all the best parts eaten and its belly full, It dug a hole in the soft dirt and buried the Claw Paw. It didn't like the taste of dirt, but most of the dirt could be shaken off and doing so made the meat last longer. Arriving at Its destination, It buried Its hands in the earth and began to dig. It was a shallow grave, only about a leg deep, but the hole had done its job. The meat was fresh and cool. The hiding hole was unmolested. It dragged the carcass out of the ditch and brushed off as much dirt from the pelt as It could.

It opened Its mouth, lowered Its head and was about to take a sizable bite out of the neck meat when It caught the smell of something on the wind. It paused, raised Its head and tested the air. Something was there. It was familiar, old thoughts and old memories. Then came the sounds of padded feet stepping through the brush. The sound of a nose pressed down low and pushing the leaves, of rapid breaths to suck the scent out of the ground itself. Then the creature came into view. It was a Pack Jaw. There was just one, but it had clearly followed the scent, which meant soon there would be others.

It snarled at the intruder, and the Pack Jaw bared its teeth, returning the aggression in kind. This wouldn't do. It was alone, It could handle a stray Pack Jaw. It focused and began to summon the light from the Slip, but the Pack Jaw threw its head to the Above and let out a long, hollow howl. Filth! Dirt in the mouth! Spoiled meat! From behind in the trees came several more howls. They were close. Frighteningly close. The Pack Jaws would have this carcass.

It threw a fallen branch at the scout and hissed Its displeasure. The limb struck the Pack Jaw across the muzzle, but it did not back down. The rest of its pack skulked out of the underbrush and formed up behind the single Pack Jaw. Together, they forced It to retreat into the night. Preoccupied with their trophy, the pack did not follow. If It got the chance, It would have to find their den, eat their young, keep the pack from growing. Pack Jaws were hard to fight. This territory was becoming hostile. For now, perhaps it was time to focus on new prey.

Eight: When It Rains

Jay sat up in his bed. It was early, the butt-crack of dawn early, but the sun was already faintly lighting up the world. Morning came a little earlier each day. It was nice having his alarm clock be a soft, blue-gold light, the songs of birds, and the occasional clatter of a pinecone hitting the metal roof. His fingers ran through his developing beard as he scratched himself. Huh, he thought. It was long enough to run fingers through. God, he was becoming a real mountain man. He didn't know how to feel about that. Jay had kept his hair buzzed short, though. Couldn't bring himself to grow out the hand holds, yet. He was putting on weight, too. By no means was he a power lifter, but his lean muscles were beginning to fill out and cover his once skeletal frame.

With a mighty yawn and a stretch he flung his legs out and got ready for the day. Tim and Earl were stirring themselves, their internal clocks rousing them from their dreams. Zack was still out cold, sprawled across his bed with disheveled sheets half hanging on the side. Jay grabbed the kid's big toe and shook it a little, saying, "C'mon, Skinny, time to adult."

Zack groaned, flopped around and pulled the covers over his head. "I don't want to adult. Bed nice. Work dumb. Stupid wolves kept me up last night, howling."

"C'mon now, up an' atom; n'less you want me to show you how to play Beat Down again."

The covers shot off Zack as he shouted and pointed accusatorially at Jay. "Fuck you, bro. I'm never forgetting that shit! That was beginners' luck, wrapped in a *chance in hell,* and deep fried in a fucking *fluke*. Hacks, I call hacks!"

Everyone chuckled and shuffled out of the bus. It was their group's turn to cook so they were up before anyone else. Like a herd of zombies, they all loaded into the kitchen and started prep. They cracked about a million eggs, and diced or grated just as many potatoes. Most of their diet at the camp was potatoes in some form or another. For the work they did it was a magical food; full of

61

vitamins, and carbs, it could be stored easily, and cooked in almost any dish. Although, they had to get creative with how to prepare them to keep things from getting repetitive.

Earl and Jay were in the back today, cooking, filling the trays, re-filling the trays, cooking some more. At least they had an arsenal of seasoning and spices. When it came to cooking Earl was a culinary wizard, and the man had a book of spells to match. The big man looked so funny hunched over a mixing bowl with a whisk, adding the perfect amount of milk, salt, butter, garlic and whatever other ingredients he decided to brew in his cauldron.

Already Jay could hear people bustling outside. They knew it was Earl's turn to cook and they were chomping at the bit.

Earl looked up from his concoction of eggs and seasonings to check up on the pan full of sliced rings of onion. "Hey, can you take those onions off? They're done caramelizing."

Jay smirked and in his thickest, heaviest Texan accent replied, "Si, señor."

The rhythmic thwacking of the whisk stopped and Earl bent over, trying his darndest to suppress a laugh as he shook his head. "That shit ain't funny. If my Grandma heard you butchering her language she'd tear you up one side and down the other."

The onions were a mouthwatering golden brown and sizzled as he took them out and began cutting them up. "Is that where you learned to cook, the School of Angry Abuela?" he said, throwing the Texas onto his Spanish as thick as he could manage.

"Seriously, I'm going to get her down here and you won't be laughing so hard, you damn smug southern boy," he said with a smile as he poured the eggy soup into a pan. It hissed and sizzled aggressively for a moment before settling down and he continued to stir them with the whisk while they scrambled. The aroma filled the kitchen and while he stirred the pan, Jay began sliding the onions into the delicious mess. "But yes, she taught me to cook. She basically lived in the kitchen. That woman, I loved her so much. I spent a lot of time with her, trying to sneak a taste of whatever she was making. She taught me all her secrets, even while I was a fat little kid who couldn't look over the counter."

"I'm just tryin' ta picture a little butterball runnin' inside from playing outdoors, 'cept I can't imagine you runnin'."

"Oh, buddy, I can run. I'm a big guy, but I can move; and dance, and *boy* can I kick. At my old work I was a Left Inside Forward on our soccer team. Sometimes when I'd go for the goal, I'd just aim for the goalie and knock him in with the ball."

"Oh yeah? Where'd you work?"

"Mart-Tropolis. I was a store director. I was in charge of a lot of stuff, but I managed it well, along with the team leads I had. It was a little hectic because all the big departments had their own teams and team leads. Then the small departments just joined into them. Large teams with little fragments to manage, but that's just Corporate sticking their nose where it doesn't belong. Anyway, out behind the store there was a field, so it was easy to get departments together and play each other."

"Huh, don't usually hear about a big wig going to prison. What happened? If'n you don't mind me askin'. They catch you stealing cheese out the backroom?"

Earl scoffed. "No. They never found out about that," he said with a wink, "my story isn't anything, really. We had just finished up the last game of our season, both teams went out drinking to celebrate. I guess they were having some redneck square dance night at the place we went to, and a bunch of Mexican Americans buying drinks and laughing in the corner just wouldn't sit right with their fragile sensibilities. So they come up and start harassing us, we tried to blow it off; even offer to buy them a round, trying to make nice. One of their drunk asses trips over himself pointing and screaming at us and thinks he was pushed. So a fight breaks out, makes the news, my job finds out, fires me for being a bad image and now I'm here. How about yourself?"

Jay should have expected the question, but it still caught him off guard. A bit flustered, he mumbled, "Money was tight. Robbed a bank."

"Robbed a bank! Hell, I figured you rustled some cattle or something. Although I guess a bank robbery does fit the whole 'Texas outlaw' thing. Did you use a six shooter and tell them to reach for the sky? Ride away on a pale horse into the sunset?"

Jay laughed nervously while Earl chuckled to himself, far too amused with his own jokes. They eventually finished up breakfast and cleaned up the aftermath. Once everything was washed and put away, the team went and got ready for the long day ahead of them. Zack and Tim had finished up and headed out as a wave of grey clouds could be seen sneaking in overhead. Their long tips reached out like tentacles across the sky to drag their behemoth body over the world.

Jay was eyeing the ominous clouds slithering through the blue sky. "Hey, you're from 'round here. Are the summer storms anything like back home?"

Earl grunted as he stuffed himself into a pair of enormous boots with spikes on the sides for climbing. "I guess that depends on what the storms are like back home."

Jay laced up his own boots and thought back. "Well, back when I was a youngin' I could go whole summers without takin' a bath, which was nice 'cause we di'n have runnin' water most of the time. The rain came down in buckets; fat drops of water pourin' down like mad. It was nice and warm, like a shower. I'd just grab the soap an' run around in it till I was clean; from the ankles up, anyway. And the lightnin'; thunderous stuff that shook you to your bones."

With a moan Earl stood up, slid on his waist harness and began to fasten it. "Well here it's damn cold. We get arctic winds from Alaska that swoop in sometimes. The rain drops aren't big, but it can pour; or drizzle, or sprinkle, or hail, then get sunny; all in the span of about ten minutes. I guess sometimes we get thunder and lightning." With a glance up skyward he gave a little, "Huh, I guess you'll see soon enough. My oldest, she hates thunder. Her and her sister share a room and every time there's a big storm I'll peek in and make sure she's doing ok. I'll usually find her all wrapped up with her little sister, sleeping like angels."

"Yeah? How old are they?"

"Mariah's thirteen, Raquel is eight. It's always so cute when she tries to take care of her big sister. Mariah, she's smart, but she needs to stand up for herself more. She'll get there, though." He flexed a truly impressive bicep and grinned. "She'll grow up as strong as her old man."

The two of them headed out as the grey, misty smog darkened the world. Shadows moved over the sun and the skies bent the light into a garish, diffuse nightmare. The stinging light twisted into his eyes and gave him a piercing headache. By the time they arrived at the work site, the clouds had opened up. It had begun.

Curtains of rain fell on them and drenched their shoulders, which their padded clothing soaked up like a sponge. It started with little more than a mist falling, but little by little it worsened to true rain; quicker than he ever would have expected. The falling spray then evolved into a downpour, with a hundred million drops of water drumming against the world in a cacophony that had to shout over to be heard.

Each step squished into the mud. The rain churned up the earth even more and scattered a deeply earthy odor with a touch of pine into the air. The longer the rain fell, the more overpowering the earthen smell became until he was nearly choking on them. He was sure by the end of the day he'd be coughing up mud.

It was his job to go along the hill and mark the trees with bright tape and perform the side cut to determine which way the tree would fall. Mat had, in the end, implemented the buddy system, and Jay's buddy, Pharrell, would come up and perform the back cut to fell the tree. Normally it was a one man job, but these were dangerous times and Mat wouldn't budge.

This kind of work wasn't easy, even on the best of days. Working on the slope was probably the most awkward way to work since he had to constantly correct his balance if he slipped or if the ground gave out under him. At times his feet sunk so deep that the mud peeked over the rim of his boot and dropped in. All the while, he kept an eye out for snag branches above him, along with his footing beneath him, all while hauling a pack full of the supplies he'd need to work out in the field. Spare gas cans with gasoline for the chainsaw, water, food, and a handful of other tools and necessities. Then of course there was the chainsaw itself. It was only a modest twenty pounds or so, but dragging that thing around all day, holding its teeth against trees while it bit and bucked, lugging it up and down the slope. It was all beginning to take its toll.

His grip on the bucking chainsaw was hard to keep as sheaths of water poured over him. The storm pounded against his hard hat like a woodpecker. He continued to wrestle with the saw for several minutes more, becoming increasingly frustrated with the uncooperative tool.

There was a knot in the wood that caused the chainsaw to bite in and get stuck. Like a dog with a bone, it bit hard and refused to let go. With a frustrated roar Jay planted one foot on the trunk and the other deep into the mud. He grit his teeth and wrenched, utilizing his whole body to lay into the machine. The mechanical teeth loosened and the jaws of the tool released, causing the serrated chain to fly past his face so closely he could feel the wind pass his nose. Had it hit him, it would have clamped onto his skull and torn him to pieces. Fortunately, he had fifty pounds of equipment strapped to his back. The extra weight had thrown him off balance which sent him sprawling into the mud.

Laying spread eagle in the mud and rain was the straw that broke the camel's back. His frustrations boiled over into rage. He'd been late for work, he was soaked to the bone, he was cold, hungry, in the middle of nowhere a million miles from home because of one fucking mistake, but what did he care? He fucking hated his home anyway, and now he had twenty pounds of mud and deer shit smeared over every inch of his body. His muscles were tired from fighting with the saw, and to pile it on even more, the rain began to fall harder and pelt his face with an unrelenting waterfall. Jay thrashed angrily until he managed to roll over and stand up. He ripped off his hard hat and furiously beat the tree with it while screaming at the world in an incoherent, mindless rage.

Pharrell wasn't too far behind and hiked over. He took off his ear muffs so he could hear, and when he spoke he had to yell to be heard over the storm. "Hey, Jay man, you doin' ok?"

Pharrell stood a little taller than Jay and was somewhere in his thirties. His skin was the color of bronzed hazel and as rich as dark chocolate, and his face was sprinkled with a handful of long healed scars. He kept his hair buzzed short around his scalp and he grew a goatee of the same length. His lean body almost made his skin look tight over his muscles, but by far the feature that Jay noticed was his big puppy eyes. God damn him, no one could stay mad with those sad marbles staring at them all concerned. In the low light, aided by the darkened sky, his marble skin seemed to disappear, giving the illusion that there were only a pair of worried eyes staring out, looking like they were about to tear up if you didn't say you were ok.

Jay hung his head and rubbed the back of his neck while he groaned in frustration. "Yeah, brother, 'M fine. I just fell, is all."

"You're sure? Because we don't cut down trees with our hats, you're not hurt or anything?"

"Nah, nah, I just lost my cool. I'm better. Let's get this done so we can pack up."

"If you're sure you're good. And remember to get that bucket back on, we don't need an old snag taking you out."

Jay looked up into the branches that swayed wildly in the wind. "No, we don't."

They got back to work and Jay forced himself to channel his anger down different avenues. He practiced some breathing exercises, but what really helped take the edge off was imagining that the trees could feel pain. After a while, Jay was able to hit a good rhythm, all things considered. They finished their partial cut of the slope which would allow the forest to regenerate without replanting. No one was up for trying to plant on a damn slope. With a job well done, they sloshed back down while other teams moved in to collect the fallen logs. The two of them made their soggy way over to a stump under the cover of a neighboring tree where they set up for lunch.

The rain had let up some, merely drizzled lightly, which was nice because having a soggy sandwich was a hellish experience. They ate while they talked each other up. They mostly just complained about the mud and the rain and how they couldn't wait to get their boots off. Near the end of their meal, someone shouting caught their attention. Finding the source wasn't hard as Mclean was leaned out the cab of his harvester and bellowed, "Get that shit out of my damn way, you retarded fucks!" Apparently he was inconvenienced by the men around him doing their jobs and clearing the fallen trees.

Jay's lunch soured in his mouth as he chewed. With the back of his hand he cuffed Pharrell on the arm and pointed toward Mclean. "How in the sam hell do you put up with that guy? I think if I was roomin' with him I'd-a kilt 'em by now."

"Charlie? He's not so bad once you get to know him. *If* you get to know him. Most people don't give him a chance, but I'll be the first to admit he's not exactly a people person."

"Hold on a hot minute. 'Charlie'?"

"Well, his name's Charles, but he was Charlie when I met him."

"And yer damn right he's not a people person. That racist, homo hatin', pinheaded man-baby ain't barely people in my book. I seen plenty of that growin' up. Now that I'm really thinkin' 'bout it, how the hell *does* he live with you? If I'm honest, I worry for you sometimes; you two bein' the only ones in your bus. It's too easy to picture wakin' up one day and find out he used your brain to repaint the walls 'cause you looked at him wrong."

Pharrell sat for a long moment, looking out toward Mclean. "No," he said after a while, "he's definitely got his problems, but he'd never hurt me. We've survived too much together."

"Prison?"

"Yeah, and some shit before that, too. In the joint we couldn't be seen talking or nothing or else we'd lose the protection of our gangs; you know how it is, you stick to your color, but we'd watch each other's backs. Get word to the other if someone was out for us, or if something big was about to go down. We survived because of each other."

Jay grumbled, not really agreeing. "I guess if you want to risk your life with that volcano, then you can call yourself Pompeii all you like."

Pharrell sat, nodding his head for a short while. "I know what it looks like from the outside, but I've seen him at his worst, and I've seen him at his best. I trust him."

After a while Jay asked, "He's got an awful lot of hair for a skinhead. What's that about?"

Pharrell laughed through his nose. "No, he's no skinhead. He was in with a biker gang and they had people on the inside, so he just slipped in with them. I knew some people from my banger days so I had a crew. I did some stuff I'm not proud of, but I survived."

Jay sat for a moment before replying, "I knew a guy in a biker gang when I was locked up. He had a limp too. I di'n care for that guy much either; not a fan of bikers." With that, he'd said all there was to say. There was an awkward silence while they finished their lunch. When they were done, they packed on their gear and headed to their new site. It was a new slope that was a bit farther down the mountain.

After downing a few trees Jay noticed his saw chain coming loose. Nothing dangerous yet, but this wasn't a tool you wanted to gamble with. If it came off it could turn his leg into ground beef or swipe his face clean off. He got some tools out of his harness and began tightening everything up. While he worked he stole a glance toward Mclean, who was driving the harvester on the ledge above their slope.

Jay took out his radio and switched to the vehicle operators channel. In his most professional voice he radioed, "Harvester One, just informin' you that there are workers below you on the slope.

69

Please acknowledge and refrain from operatin' the vehicle in the area until we've cleared." Jay knew to hold the radio back a bit once he'd finished.

The response was so blown out that it was hard to decipher words from it, but it was clear enough. "I fucking know you're down there, you panty waist pussy. Do you want me to send down some toilet paper? 'Cause you're crying at me like you shit yourself, scared."

Jay tried to resist the temptation, but he just couldn't help himself. "Negative, Harvester One, keep the toilet paper up top. Sounds like your mouth needs it more'n my ass."

Jay held the radio even farther away and slipped his ear muffs back on, waiting for the retaliatory onslaught of abuse, but strangely, there was radio silence. With a shrug, he put the radio back on his belt, hefted the chainsaw up, and went back to work. He was tying the tree with marker tape when he felt something sprinkle onto the back of his neck and bounce off his helmet. Thinking a snag had come loose and was about to come crashing down, he panicked and jumped back, but when he looked up it was something much worse. The harvester was holding a log over the slope and "processing it". Strips of bark, clumps of dirt and rock and entire branches were raining down on him. That out of control, swamp brained, throwback was going to kill him!

Jay cupped his head in his hands and launched himself down the slope. Balled up in a tuck and roll position, he tumbled down the steep embankment at a terrifying speed. As he sped down the mountain, he heard a mighty crash behind him. As he tumbled down the hill, branches and twigs from bushes whipped his skin and clawed at his clothes, but his thick work gear defended him from the worst of it; until he came to a crushing stop. He impacted against a tree so hard that the wind was knocked out of him. He knew immediately that it was going to bruise, and he hoped he hadn't broken or cracked any of his ribs. The impact bounced him off the trunk like a rubber ball and he continued his descent.

Mercifully, he soon came to rest at the bottom and uncurled like a pill bug on its back. He took a breath and gave himself a careful once over. He could see straight, which meant he didn't hit his head. He didn't feel any shooting, terrible pain so probably nothing had broken, but that might just be adrenaline; he had better be careful when he stood up. He sat up and felt fine for a man who just fell off a mountain, so he leaned on an arm in an attempt to stand. Instantly he recoiled in pain. He looked down and discovered there was a small branch poking through his padded work shirt. He tried to pull it out, but it sent a bolt of pain through him that radiated throughout his whole body.

After gingerly examining it more, he realized what he was looking at. He had been impaled by a spike of wood. Not seriously, it seemed, but from how it looked he guessed it had just caught the skin below his ribs, right in the soft spot between the ribs and hips. It wasn't a serious injury compared to what it could have been, but it was serious enough. An inch or two to the left and who knows what it might have hit. Doctors would know, he guessed. Jay began going over his options in his mind. Taking it out would have been just about the dumbest thing to do, so he grit his teeth and lurched out of the mud. His shirt and coat were beginning to soak with red.

Pharrell had seen him tumble and shouted down at him, "Jay, how are you doing down there? Are you ok?"

Jay looked back at his fall. It seemed like he'd fallen much farther than how it felt. His equipment was scattered all down the slope, but he was glad he had jumped. The place where he was standing before was under an entire tree, snapped in half and splintered at one end. He turned, with some effort, toward Pharrell and called back, "Get the medical bag, I need some patching up." Jay carefully took a seat on a stump and waited for Pharrell.

Pharrell came down quickly with a small red bag filled with various first aid supplies. They had to cut the shirt a bit so Pharrell could work around the wound. It wasn't a deep wound, and just as Jay had suspected, it had only caught the skin, but it was going to leave two holes in him and it was the exact opposite of pleasant.

Pharrell readied some folded medical cloth on some tape and gave it to Jay to hold. "Ok, on the count of three, I'm going to pull the branch out and then you're going to get that pad on there quick. You ready?"

Jay set his jaw, closed his eyes and nodded.

Taking the back of the branch in his hand Pharrell said, "Ok, on three." Then without warning he slid it out with speed. The spike slid out smoothly and Pharrell quickly guided Jay's hand, along with the bandage, to the wound as Jay doubled over and groaned like he'd just been kicked.

Whipping his head around, Jay shot daggers at him.

Pharrell just shrugged. "Couldn't have you tensing up. Might have torn something when it came out."

Unable to properly argue the point, Jay settled for shaking his head and trying to forget about the throbbing impalement that was in his side. After some applied pressure, disinfectant, and lots of medical tape, they were able to stop the bleeding and dress the wound. It would have to be sewn shut later, after it had been properly cleaned and redressed.

He was still able to walk, albeit with a small bit of trouble, and declined any help getting back to camp. Somebody volunteered to take his equipment back with them, but he honestly didn't remember who. He was too deep in his own thoughts, plotting.

— — — — — — — — — —

It took longer than he would have liked, but he made it back to camp without help. He stripped off his remaining mud caked clothing and took a shower, carefully making sure to scrub off as best he could, considering his stab wound. The two holes in his side didn't impede him as much as he'd expected, but God be damned, it hurt like hell.

After losing ten pounds of blood flavored mud, he walked naked back to the bus and put fresh bandages on. Then he threw on his comfort clothes; black sweatpants, a red plaid long sleeve shirt, and bare feet. He had kept the splintered spike and laid it down on his small end table. Above his bed, Jay had taken off the door to one of the cabinets. He had taken to carving in his free time and used the shelf like a little display case. The miniature show room was filled with little statuettes of animals, some were local, others were from far off places; places he'd only ever heard about or seen on T.V. The creatures in the menagerie were roughly shaped, but recognizable; more so with each piece he completed. Jay grabbed his wooden stake and opened the back door of the bus. Letting his legs hang out, he began to swing them a little while he carved the spike with his tiger handled pocket knife. The old man was right, it didn't hold an edge long, but there were plenty of opportunities to sharpen blades at a logging camp.

He whittled on for a long time, shaping the wood, letting himself get absorbed into his work to distract from his frustrations. He didn't know how long he had zoned out, but there was a healthy pile of wood shavings between his feet when the explosive sound of a door slamming ripped through the silence and startled him aware. The long antenna on Mat's trailer shook as he stomped out. Without breaking stride he picked up a large ax and began furiously attacking a nearby stump. With each swing he sent shrapnel and debris exploding out as he chopped.

Jay set the little wooden cat down and made sure to close the door to the bus; he didn't want some critter getting in and chewing up the place. He pocketed the knife and walked over to his ax wielding maniac of a friend, careful not to reopen his wound as he walked. With a wry smile he spread his arms and called out, "Need a pat, Mat?"

Snapping up, Mat quickly softened. He gave the log one more blow and buried the ax deep into the center ring. The big man trampled over and embraced his friend and gave him several good smacks on the back, "Do *I* need a pat? My god damn friends are getting stabbed, and they're asking if *I'm* ok? Stupid asshole."

"Eh, it's just a flesh wound."

With an indignant snort Mat chuckled. "Ok, Black Knight." Then he let out a long, frustrated sigh and said, "I got updated over the radio, and I just got off the SAT phone with my lawyer. I gave him a rundown of what happened. He says that because 'the injury' happened because of your dive off the cliff, a good lawyer could argue that you're the one at fault. Plus, that gang he's in has some very good lawyers. They could even sue if we decide to terminate the contract. He said we'd win if they did, but it would be a 'pyrrhic victory' and we'd be better off just paying out. I told that book worm that he was more worm than book, and that I'd be seeking other legal advice."

"Yeah, I figure you knew better'un me what's been going on, but the things you was tellin' me di'n seem on the up and up."

"Watch, we'll start digging and find out he was being bribed or something. Fucking Mclean. Before I fired him, the old manager hired Mclean and then he transferred here. Well, the contract the guy wrote up basically says if we fire him, he can take us for all we're worth. I'm pretty sure that guy spent a lot of time in the prison library reading up on legalese." Mat rolled his head back and gave a long, throaty, frustrated sigh. "If I thought it'd make anything better I'd be tempted to just break out the rifle and shoot the bastard myself."

At the mention of the firearm Jay perked up a bit. "We've got guns here?" Then he paused and thought for a second. "That don't seem like the best thing to have 'round convicts."

"It's just for emergencies; bears or something, and it's in a safe. Combinations only in my head," he said, but as he said it he seemed to pause a moment and look up, thinking, before glancing at Jay and shaking the thought off, "anyway, how are you holding up?"

Lifting his shirt Jay showed off his battle damage. "Gonna get a kick ass scar for my trouble. Damn stick stabbed right through the work jacket, and that thing's thicker'n a Texas family at an all you can eat buffet."

Mat could only smile and cross his arms as he thought back to old times. "I fucking missed those little Texas-isms. Well, if you're not gonna die on me then I guess I can start making some calls. I've got a lawyer to find. We'll put you on chainsaw sharpening duty for a few days so you don't miss any work."

With a shrug and a wince Jay responded, "Sounds fine to me. I'll let you get goin' then. I'll keep busy."

They parted ways and returned to their respective lodges. Jay picked up the little wooden cat and heard the door of the trailer closing, this time infinitely more gently. After a time, people began to trickle back into camp while Jay gave his tiger its stripes.

* * * * * * * * *

The Sun was leaving the world. It flew far over the forest to its den. It wondered what the Sun's den looked like. It was probably awful. The Night Sun would awaken soon. The thought of being able to prowl the night made It happy. Little else did. A gust of wind pushed on Its back. Its grip tightened around the branch that It crouched upon. It was brooding, far from where the Pack Jaws could disturb It. It had been too long since It had eaten. The Pack Jaws were eating Its meat, and if It wasn't careful It would become their meat. It unconsciously bared Its teeth at the thought.

It was hungry and ready for a hunt. It sniffed the air, sampling the wind. Then, good smell. Very good! The good smell washed over it like an intoxicating wave. Its eyes bulged, the pupils dilated. It became excited and sniffed at the air like the Pack Jaws, trying to find the good smell. With anticipation fit to burst, It crawled down the tree and charged off in the direction of the loud Tall Ones territory.

It had been days since It had eaten and there were too many Tall Ones in its hunting grounds. It liked Tall Ones, when they were alone. They were slow, and they tasted of salt and fat. So much fat. Sometimes mouthfuls of it! The more fat, the slower the Tall One was. They were the best prey, but It didn't like the smell of the loud Tall One's territory. It smelled like blackness and poison, and the air was rough. The last one It got from there was foul, even though it was fresh, but hunger is a master convincer, and the fat was still good. Drooling, It charged between trees, down slopes, up cliffs, and over boulders like they weren't even there.

It only slowed down as it entered the loud Tall Ones territory. The area reeked of musk, urine, and Black Poison. There were many males and they marked frequently, but above the whirlwind of scents, it was able to cut straight to the good smell. There it was, smeared against the base of a tree, and then down the hill.

Blood. Fresh. Trail. That way.

Nine: When Lions Roar

Jay grunted as he seated himself at the table. His wound was healing fast. He chalked it up to how quickly it had been cleaned and the treatment afterward. He pulled a bowl of mac and cheese under his nose and breathed in its scent. It was an aromatic symphony of delight. He barely stopped himself from drooling as he cracked the bread crumble crust that had been toasted to a golden brown. He moaned with pleasure as the flavor of several melted cheeses washed over his pallet. Then the chili layer underneath hit and the ingredients mixed and danced on his taste buds. "This; I fuckin' *needed* this. Who's on mess tonight? Greg? Remind me to kiss that beautiful bastard. God bless 'em."

Zack poked at his side and chided, "Is that where Mother Nature shanked you? I'll bet you're just faking to get on light duty, you faker."

Jay pointed his spoon threateningly. "Young'n, if you interrupt daddy's chili mac dinner I *will* put you into an early grave."

With an impish grin Zack retreated out of spoon range and began to dig into his own bowl. After a few bites that decimated about half of the bowl, he nodded in agreement. "Ok, Gregory's a fuckin' angel and he deserves a pimp chalice for this shit. No, something better! We're unworthy."

Tim and Earl sat down with them and all four of their bowls disappeared quickly. They stacked them high in the center and just sat comfortably, chatting.

Tim was regaling them with an epic tale of two squirrels he saw that day who had been fighting over a pine cone. "So then the big brown loses the grey tail around a tree, and runs off to bury the damn thing. He starts digging the hole, and wouldn't you know it, a bald-fucking-eagle comes *right* down and gets the little critter! Then! Then, the grey tail comes over and steals it back!"

Tim erupted into laughter and was joined in by everyone at the table. It was strange, then, that without warning his mood soured. The joy left his eyes and they were flooded with smoldering murder. He put his hands flat on the table and began to stand.

Jay followed his gaze and spied Mclean. He'd gotten his food and was walking to his normal table with Pharrell. Mclean was sporting nothing more than a tank top, jeans, and boots. He saw Tim and began to stalk over. With an expression like he was sucking on a lemon, he glowered down at them and rumbled, "You got something to fucking say to me, cunt?"

Jay put his hand on Tim's shoulder and eased him down, then said, "Just keep walkin', Mclean."

The Sasquatch slowly turned his head and set his jaw. They locked eyes and he slammed his bowl down as he leaned forward with both firsts on the table, flexing his gigantic, fur carpet arms. "What are you and that black tar sucking bitch going to do; glitter bomb me? Here's some advice, faggot. If sex is a pain the ass, you're doing it wrong."

Jay locked his jaw, and the two of them locked eyes. "I said just keep walkin', **Mclean**."

With the fakest, most condescending voice that had ever been spoken, Mclean put one hand over his heart and said, "Aw, did I hurt your little feelings? I'm *sorry*. Tell you what, why don't we lighten things up a bit. I know, how about a joke? Besides the one in your mirror. Why are gays happy that they have nutsacks?" He just stood there and let an ogre grin slip onto his face, "Queers have nutsacks because they use them as mud flaps."

As Mclean leaned forward, his massive deltoid rolled forward with him. Mclean didn't usually wear tank tops, and Jay usually paid him as much attention as a pile of dogshit, but tonight he finally got a good look at the fiery tattoo on the man's shoulder. It was a stylized, roaring lion with a mane made out of living fire. It was at that moment that several pieces fell into place. Jay spoke slowly and tensed his body, "Last chance, Mclean."

The larger man just glowered down at him and growled, "You didn't laugh at my joke."

Jay shot to his feet and mirrored Mclean. There was so much friction between the two, their gaze could have started a wildfire. In a bone dry deadpan Jay spat, "How's that knee doin', Mclean?"

The grin drained from his face in an instant. The big man leaned back and lumbered around the table until his hairy chest was in Jay's face. "The fuck did you say to me, little man?"

Never breaking his gaze he replied, "Back home I bunked with a fella'; had a tattoo that looked an awful lot like yours. Said he was in the Hellfire Pride, a biker gang from around these parts. Thing is, he walked with a limp, this guy. So one night he's drunk on toilet wine and tar and I ask him about it. I guess a guard's sister got kilt and they di'n take too kindly to the Pride. They'd bust up members every chance they got, starting with the knee. Now, 'big man', unless you go have a seat all peaceful like with your boyfriend over there, I'm goin' to drop you at the knee and kick your goddamn *teeth* in. And I won't be alone. Who do you got?"

Mclean looked like he could shoot rays of death itself from his eyes, but he clearly didn't like the position he was in. He glanced over at Pharrell who was just sitting at the table, watching, worried at the exchange. If looks could kill, Mclean would never see the light of day for the murder in his eyes was unquenchable. His fists were white at the knuckles, and his arms trembled with how tense he flexed them; not helped in the least by the adrenaline his body injected through his veins. His face contorted and it looked like he was about to make a move, but one look at Tim, who was already standing, and a glance at Earl who was slowly rising, himself, made Mclean think twice. He spit on Jay's shirt and with one more, sour look to each of them he turned, the giant stomped off into the night. He violently crushed his foot into the ground and exploded the mud with every step.

It startled everyone when Pharrell's voice sheepishly broke the silence. He was standing there with his head hung, looking like a kicked puppy. "I'm sorry. I don't mean to make excuses for him, but he never really got out, you know? To him, everything is still life or death. I hope you guys have a good night." And with that he

79

scooped up their small tower of bowls and took them over to the food bus before he retired for the night.

Jay's arms were trembling from the adrenaline wearing off and he was trying to slow down his racing heart.

Tim gave a gravelly cackle and slapped him hard on the back. "Ho-ly-shit, that was just about the most spectacular thing I've *ever* seen, and I've seen six tons of ordnance go up in a single day!"

All he could manage as a response was a halfhearted laugh and an up nod while he continued to try and come down from the buildup.

Earl slid Mclean's uneaten bowl toward himself and began to dig in. He demolished the bowl and stood up to give his own back slaps. "Tell you what, it's been one hell of a day, let's head back, maybe put our feet up and play some cards?"

Zack was grinning ear to ear as he bounced in his seat and shadow boxed with excitement. "Shit, son, that was so *dope*! D'you see his *face*? He walks up on us tryin' to flex. Then he be all like, 'Ahhgh *fuck*, I messed with the wrong *crew*!'"

A nod of heads and the four retired to their bus as well. Jay flopped down onto his bed and tried to relax. Tim and Earl sat at the little table and took out a deck of cards and started shuffling.

Zack took up his seat in front of the T.V, turned on a computer and shuffled through an external hard drive of T.V shows and movies. "Anybody know what they want?"

Without looking up from his hand Tim replied, "Just none of that crazy cartoon shit. Hurts my head; and my eyes. Oh! How about that one where they make the animal jaws, put them on little RC tanks and make them fight!"

"Mechanical Maws it is."

* * * * * * * * *

Mclean was still seething with malice and hate. That *fucking* little shit heel was going to cost him his Job, and he couldn't go back to prison. He'd kill himself before he went back to that fucking pit. He stomped around in the dark, the light of the camp far, far to his back.

There was a half-moon high in the sky. It shed enough light to see shadows and shapes in the soggy night. There were no clouds now, and the night was brisk. The smell of rain, fresh dirt and moisture filled the air, but it did precious little to temper or cool his pyroclastic anger.

He grabbed a hefty branch from the ground and with a guttural bellow he smashed it into a tree like a baseball bat, over and over and over until it splintered, crumbled, and flew off into the dark, a broken and mangled wreck of wood pulp.

Breathing heavily, he fell to his knees and punched the ground. Between clenched teeth he screamed, deep in his throat. He punched the ground again before sitting back and turning toward the sky.

The sky. All that space beyond this shitty little rock. Lit up by a single light bulb that would burn out one day. What did it matter? What did *he* matter? He was a fuck up, he was the exact thing every one said he'd be. A disappointment, a freak, a criminal, a complete and *total* failure. Nothing he did would leave any kind of mark unless it was a scar. Nothing he'd ever do would matter.

And that fucking little *SHIT* saw right through him. The memory caused every insecurity to come rocketing to the surface. He sat in the mud, crying, caught between staring up at the stars or down into the dirt. He sat until his legs hurt, the twigs and rocks digging into his knees and legs. He didn't care. He'd had worse done to him since before he could stand. The night was quiet, with the only exception being the soft hooting of an owl in the distance and the rustle of branches in the wind. It sounded like the distant roar of the ocean. He'd never been to the ocean, but he'd seen it on T.V.

Maybe once he'd saved enough money. Maybe once his parole was over and he could leave the state, he'd go get his old bike. Then he'd buy a second one, and him and Pharrell would ride

81

to California. Hell, maybe even Mexico; or farther! They'd drive the long way, all the way along the ocean, smelling the sea and eating at all the little dive bars. Just get away somewhere. Somewhere with a beach by the ocean; and he could put this whole place behind him.

A snapped twig ripped him right back to earth. He shot up, wincing at the pain in his knee. Instinctually his fists shot up, ready to fucking *kill* whoever was dumb enough to *fuck* with him.

But, there was nothing. At least, nothing that he understood. It was beautiful though; the light. The warm, yellow ball, so delicately pulsing as it hovered in the tree line. It was so dim that he wasn't sure if he even really saw it, but he felt good. Very good! And so calm. It felt like someone was standing behind him and touching his skull just behind his ears; touching with only their fingertips while they massaged the soft spots of his head. His eyes went out of focus. His head bowed a little and he slowly, calmly, walked toward the light. He hoped he could feel like this forever. After just a few moments, or maybe it was a few hours, he finally caught up to the light. He came up close to it, letting the sensation of coziness wrap itself around him like a warm blanket.

With eyes half lidded and mouth smiling wide, his vision drank deep at the pool of enticing light. It continued to throb in even, rhythmic pulses. The warm feeling washed over him again and raised him up with each pulse, pushing and pulling him, ebbing and flowing like the tides of the ocean.

With the dazed, slurred words of a man inebriated, he greeted his new friend, "Hello, buddy."

The light was polite. In a raspy, strained voice it replied, "Hhhehahlloo, buuugh dee."

Ten: Following Footsteps

Mat snorted awake, rudely torn from his pleasant dreams by a mad pounding on his trailer door. The tragedy compounded as the last wisps of memory about the curvaceous woman he'd been "entertaining" left his mind. Another round of banging bombarded his door.

Stuffing himself into his boxer shorts he threw on a pair of jeans and threaded a belt through it. He adjusted himself as best he could and cinched the belt tight to hold everything in place. All the while he muttered curses and promises of wrath and retribution if this wasn't the worst damn thing to happen on the whole planet. A third round of banging assaulted the flimsy trailer door.

With a roar, Mat screamed back, "Just a goddamn second, let a man dress himself."

Through the door came the muffled, but clearly concerned voice of Pharrell. "Mat, Mat I need to talk to you! It's about Mclean!"

Mat visibly slumped. Great, what happened now? He could have been face deep into a pair of melon sized melons right now, but instead he was dealing with Mclean's shit. He skipped putting on a proper shirt, opting for a long jacket to try and help cover up his morning wood. Still half asleep, but fully enraged he threw open the door and glowered down at the Wrecker of Sexy-Time Dreams. **"What**?"

Pharrell looked up at him with those god damn puppy eyes. The morning was still cool, but he was already sweating and he was clearly trying to catch his breath. "Mclean didn't come back last night."

Rubbing the sleep from his eyes, Mat looked past him into the camp. It was still dark out, but toward the horizon the black of night was beginning to give way to a little smudge of blue. It was deep into summer and the mornings started early now. Mat looked at his watch on the counter, and growled at the time. "Pharrell, it is exactly Fuck-You-O'clock in the morning and I was... sleeping *very* well. What is so goddamn important? So what if that ogre decided to eat dirt all night instead of dinner?"

"No, I mean he didn't come back *at all*. He's not in camp. He had a fight with Jay and Tim last night and stomped off. I figured he'd blow off some steam, but I woke up and he still wasn't there. I've been running all over camp trying to find him!"

With a long sigh, Mat pinched the bridge of his nose and leaned against the doorway. He thought for a moment while he scraped the sleep from the corners of his eye. "Ok, look man, the sun's not even up yet, everyone's still asleep and it's Mclean we're talking about. The man could fist fight a bear and win. If he's not back by the time his shift starts, then I'll see what we can do about finding him. I think Earl has some experience tracking. Until then, get some sleep." With a wide yawn Mat shut the door on his uninvited guest and flopped back down on his bed to try and summon his illusive beauty again.

– – – – – – – – – –

About an hour and some change later his alarm went off, telling him to get up and get to work. He groaned and punched the off button. With a slurred, "Fugk off," he yawned wide and pushed himself up out of bed. He was breathing deep and rubbing his face when the banging returned. The air escaped through his nose in a long, exasperated sigh. He steeled himself, popped his neck, and went to the door. Without looking, he opened it and droned, "Yes, Pharrell?"

Clearly he hadn't taken Mat's advice to sleep. There were bags under his eyes and they were less puppy and more panic now. Pharrell just shrugged as he looked expectantly at Mat.

With another yawn, he rubbed the stubble on his chin and rolled his head back. "Ok, fine, come on in and tell me what happened; from the start."

———————

They had a responsibility to look after their own, for better or for worse. So after all was said and done, Mat and Earl went out to see if they could rope that son of a bitch Mclean back to camp.

The sun was up. Not terribly high, yet, but they could feel it starting to heat up. It was going to be a scorcher that day. The rest of the camp went to work like they always did while he went to play personal nanny to a ninny. So here he was, rifle in hand, just standing around while Earl played in the dirt. It was going to be one of *those* days.

Mat looked down as Earl practically laid on the ground to get an exceptionally close look at a boot print. "So, what are you doing, exactly?"

"Checking to see if it's fake."

Mat propped the gun against a tree and rolled his neck, trying to work out a kink. "Why would it be fake?"

"Mclean was pretty upset last night. For all we know he's trying to run away and doesn't want us to follow him, so maybe he made a decoy trail."

"And?"

Earl stood up and dusted off his belly and knees. "No, these are his and they're real. You can tell how the shoe moved as his foot changed weight in it. And he's a hell of a big guy, which makes this a million times easier."

"I think you're giving him too much credit, man. Mclean's a simple creature, he wouldn't plan to stomp into the woods, he'd just do it. So, which way did he stomp?"

"Well, that's the thing. Here you can see him stomping away from camp, deep boot marks with high impact ridges and some splash, then this big smudge here and that broken branch. There's no weathering on the wood, see how it's all white? That means it's been exposed to the elements recently. I'm guessing he

85

smacked a tree around, broke it, and sat down which made the smudge marks. But then he stands up and just sort of stands there for a while. These two deep prints with a clean ridge show that, but then he just, I don't know, turns into a zombie?"

That caught Mat's attention. "Say what, now?"

"I don't know, it's strange. Look," Earl said as he pointed to some long lines in the soft earth leading toward the forest, "those aren't drag marks. There's boot impressions here and there where the foot sunk in. It looks like he was dragging his feet with each step, just walking into the woods, but I don't know why he'd do that."

Mat picked up the bolt action rifle and slung it over his shoulder. "Well that just means he's walking slow and left us a trail, let's go, man."

They followed the shuffling tracks for a few miles, walking through the thick foliage, pushing through bushes and navigating the treacherous hills and valleys of the rolling mountain range. The trees were thick this far out and they loomed eerily above the two men, their presence as ominous as it was beautiful. Mat began to feel a bit claustrophobic with how tight the vegetation was beginning to get.

Time passed, but Mat was still feeling a bit squeamish under the imposing presence of the woods. The branches were low, and he had to push through them, letting his tough jacket take the brunt of the assault. He had no such protection for his psyche however. His one saving grace that kept him calm was how confident Earl was as he trudged through the northwestern jungle. Thinking some more on the matter brought up a good question, and focusing on a conversation was infinitely better than the alternative.

"Hey, Earl, back in camp when I was asking if anyone could track, you volunteered. I'm guessing you spent a lot of time outdoors?"

Earl knelt down and prodded the dirt. "Not so much. My Grandpa, though, he *lived* the outdoors. That man was tougher than iron."

Trying to distract from the quickly constricting foliage, he kept the ball rolling and asked, "Oh yeah? Was he a ranger or something?"

They were walking along a fairly even path now, and Earl wiped the sweat from his forehead and caught his breath. "Nah, he came up from South America fleeing cartels. He never said where exactly he was from, but we always guessed it was Columbia. He was a teacher down there, and ran a little school house in a village. They came to his school to take the kids, probably to get them hooked on drugs and beat them into soldiers. He let them round up the kids, cooperated with everything they told him, let them get a few hits in to let their guard down. Then he stabbed the last guy out the door in the throat with a pencil and took his gun. The way he tells it, he killed thirty men. It was probably more like three or four, but then he had to hide. He lived in the jungle, slowly working his way up to Mexico where he met my Grandma. Then he lived in the desert with her near the U.S border. He got in good with some of the border guards; always sent them good intel when he found human traffickers or drug mules in his area. Eventually he moved north and had my dad."

"Holy shit, man. All my grandpa did was die of cirrhosis. So, he was a teacher? Seems kind of, I don't know, blood thirsty? For a teacher, that is."

"He was able to teach *me* real easy. I believe he was a teacher, but he refuses to talk about anything before that. For all I know the guy was a serial killer or a guerrilla fighter. Or hell, maybe he was *in* the cartel. But yeah, he was always telling me things about how to read nature. This though...."

They stopped as Earl knelt down and examined something in one of the drag marks.

Looking around, Mat took stock of their surroundings while Earl did... whatever he was doing. "What do you got, man?"

"I thought maybe I was just seeing something, but there's definitely two sets of tracks here. Someone's walking in front of him. His feet mess up their tracks, but they're there."

Mat's blood ran cold at the sudden change of situation. Another person complicated things. Who were they? Were they always here? Did they know Mclean? Were they going to try to steal from the camp? Were they armed? No, Mat didn't like this at all. Until now he had figured Mclean was throwing a temper tantrum. If he was conspiring with his old gang, or if there were backwoods hill folk out there, they could be in real danger. "What can you tell me about them?"

Earl swept his hand over his bald head and flicked the sweat away. "That's the thing, it kind of looks like hands."

Mat swore he could feel his brain stop working for a moment. "What, so someone is doing a handstand through the woods?"

There was a long pause while Earl studied the tracks more closely. Before long he wiped more sweat from his face and nose and said, "That's what it looks like, yeah."

All Mat could do was stare stupidly at the back of Earls head so hard he feared he might burn a hole through it.

Earl turned and saw his utterly blank expression. He put his hands up and said, "Hey, I'm just telling you what it looks like. For all I know this new guy's got small feet and long toes or something. The tracks *are* messed up from Mclean dragging his house sized feet over them, so maybe he messed them up?"

Vigorously shaking off the stupid, Mat gave one more look around them and shifted his brain to high alert. "Ok, here's the plan. We keep going for a little longer and if it doesn't look like we'll find him soon, we turn back. I don't know what's going on here, but it doesn't sit well with me."

"You and me both," Earl said as he grunted and got back to his feet.

They followed the tracks on a relatively flat path for another hour before it broke into a clearing. Sweet, wonderful open space. The kind where you can see someone lurking behind you, as long as you have the wherewithal to turn your damn head. The field was mostly grass, wild, long and untamed, save for a long swath leading directly uphill into a boulder field. Even Mat knew there was almost no way to follow the trail through that.

They decided to call it a bust and turned back. The hike back to camp seemed longer, somehow. The woods had a funny way of doing that; changing space. The trees seemed to be taller, more oppressive, and darker. Yeah, it was definitely getting darker. It felt like there was a pair of eyes behind every tree, watching their every step, waiting for an opportunity, a moment of weakness to exploit.

Trying to make his voice sound calmer than he felt, Mat said, "Hey, man, I think we should pick up the pace."

Earl stopped, put his hands on his hips and leaned back a little, panting and sweating heavily. He gave Mat a look of condemnation and said, "Yeah, Mr. Athlete? Are you going to carry my fat ass back? I hang from a tree for fifteen hours a day with fifty pounds of equipment while I operate a five-foot chainsaw. I've got the strength of a horse, and the long distance speed of a turtle. So unless you've got a helicopter in your pocket..."

The two of them got a breathless chuckle at that, and Mat yielded, "Ok, horse man, but I *do* want to get back before dark. The woods are creepy enough at night without maniacs stalking in the bushes."

"Do you mean our mystery man or Mclean," Earl said with a wry smile.

Mat chuckled again and said, "Yes."

— — — — — — — — — —

They made it back to camp with too few hours of good day light left. Upon their return there was a strange hubbub. A huge crowd had formed and everyone was milling around, looking around in the dirt, or breaking off in little groups talking to each other.

Mat cut through the crowd, swinging the rifle onto his back and tightening the strap to hold it in place. He walked up to the only

89

Afghani in the camp. Muhammad would know what was going on. That schmoozer loved talking people up and made it his business to know the newest gossip. Maybe it was his small-town spirit coming to light. Mat knew how that went; there were no secrets in small towns. He approached and waved in greeting. "Moe, what's going on, man? Is Mclean back?" he asked, more hopeful than he realized.

Moe looked up from his conversation with two other men. He was a middle-aged man, thin, and had a well-kept beard and a shaved head, but one could still see where the hair tried to grow back. The man had spent the last twenty or so years in the states and spoke perfect English, albeit with a slight Middle Eastern accent that sounded almost Russian. "No, he has not come back to camp, but *something* has. There's tracks all over the camp, some tools were thrown around, but it didn't get into anything else."

"Jay should have been here on blades; did he see anything?"

"I have not talked to him yet, my friend."

Mat clapped him on the shoulder. "Thanks, man." He then walked into the crowd to try and find Jay. Everywhere he looked people were either cleaning up tools that were sprawled across the camp, checking on personal possessions to make sure they weren't stolen, or standing around and talking amongst themselves in quiet, energetic conversations.

In his search he passed by the back door of the food bus and saw one of their axes laying haphazardly on the ground, surrounded by shards of broken glass. He picked it up to help with the cleanup effort, but as he stooped down to retrieve it he noticed where the glass had come from. The window of the emergency exit had been shattered. Most of the glass had been blown inward. The ax lay on top of the glass, which confirmed that the ax was the implement of destruction.

He examined the hole, trying to think of how they could patch it until repairs could be made, when he noticed a thick line of blood dripping from a particularly pointed piece of glass, still nestled in the frame. Whoever tried to get in was hurt, at least a little. He'd have to check the arms of everyone in camp just to make sure it wasn't one of his own.

Deciding there was nothing he could do to fix the hole right now, he continued his search to find the only man who had been in camp all day. After several minutes of searching, he found Jay helping to take inventory near the gas powered angle grinder. It was housed in a little shed that had been brought in to store larger equipment.

Mat waved him over and shook the ax a little. "Got one more for you here."

Jay came over and took the tool. "Ah, good, just missing one more. I di'n know axes had legs, though. Where'd this one wander off to?"

"It was behind the Mess. The back window is busted, so we'll have to get that patched up before something gets a sniff in there. You were here all day, right?"

Scratching the back of his head Jay confessed, "Yeah, I was, but I didn't see nothin'. I was workin' the grinder all day and had ear plugs in. I'd locked the door 'cause I'm paranoid 'bout people coming up behind me. I'd wager it all happened after lunch, though, 'cause I stretched my legs for a bit and nothin' were out of place then."

Rolling his neck and groaning with frustration Mat asked, "Not anything? Nothing out the corner of your eye, no loud bang between grinds? Nothing?"

"I'm sorry, Mat, I di'n see nothin'."

He rubbed his eyes and pinched the bridge of his nose. What the hell was going on around here? Taking a deep breath and forcing himself to stay focused he just said, "It's fine. I just wish we knew more. Honestly you being here probably scared off whoever did this before they did any *real* damage. Ok, I've got to secure the rifle and call... somebody. At least let the authorities know what's happened and that we've got a worker MIA. If everything is accounted for then you can put your feet up for a while. One ax missing won't stop the whole camp. I'll probably be making an announcement tonight. See you 'round, man."

Jay nodded and tried to give a reassuring smile. "Later, brother."

—————————

Earl sat down hard in his chair while the other three men took their seats. "Well *that's* going to make things hard. I mean, the whole point of this line of work is that we're spread out. How the hell is a buddy system going to work for me? I mean, hell, am I supposed to wear my buddy like a backpack while I'm sixty feet up?"

Tim reclined on his bed and pulled out a book with the title of *The Clovis People and Their Legacy*. He flipped it open to his marked page and began reading. "Strength in numbers," he called out.

Earl rolled his eyes and said, "I *get* it, I just don't understand how most of this new stuff is actually going to *work* though."

Jay pulled up a chair and shuffled a deck of cards. "Interesting title, ol'man, what're you reading there?"

Tim grunted back, "Clovis people. Natives round here during mammoth times. Fascinating stuff. Bunch of it's only come out in the last couple years. You should give it a read once I'm done."

"I'll do that," he said before he chimed back in on the original discussion while he dealt himself a round of solitaire, "But the buddy system, honestly, that's probably the least of our worries. The whole camps speculatin' 'bout Mclean an' I don't think a one of 'em believe he's alive. From cougars, to falling down a mountain. Hell, Greg thinks he got ate by a Bigfoot. I think the man should stick to cookin'."

A sound effect of metal clashing against metal echoed from the television as Zack put on an episode of *Mechanical Maws*.

Tim looked up from his book and called out, "Hey, Skinny, what animals are on this one?"

"Umm, saltwater crocodile vs a great white shark. My money's on the shark."

"Agh," Tim scoffed in his throaty way, "croc will tear that thing apart."

The two argued in the background, even putting money down on who they thought would win. Earl leaned in over the table toward Jay. "Honestly, that bigfoot thing might not be far off."

Jay looked up from his cards and gave him a confused look. "I di'n take you for a believer."

"So you know how me and Mat went out looking for Mclean? Well following him was easy, but there was something else with him. I don't know what it was, but it didn't wear shoes and it was heavy. If I'm being honest, I don't think it was a person. The track was all wrong and it was deep enough to survive being walked over by Mclean; he's no featherweight. He was walking real funny, too, dragging his feet."

Jay looked him dead in the eye and smirked, raising an eyebrow.

"Ok, he was walking funnier than *usual*, smart guy. My point is this whole thing is a special kind of weird."

Jay played a few cards while he thought. "And you think it's Bigfoot?"

"No, that shit isn't real."

Zack half turned and called over his shoulder, "Bro, Bigfoot is *so* real. That video of it walking by the river was picked apart and if it's a guy in a suit, than it's the best suit ever made and the guy wearing it has stupid long arms. Bigfoot is real, dude."

Ignoring him, Earl turned back to his conversation. "This whole thing stinks of something... something else. Something God rebuked long ago."

Jay dropped his hands hard on the table and gave Earl the most dumbfounded-est look he could muster. "Ex-cuse me?"

Earl leaned in closer, his voice barely louder than a whisper. "Demons, man. I think it might be a demon."

Still wearing his astounded face, Jay asked in a deadpan, "I don't know 'bout no Bigfoot, but I can tell you it ain't no demon."

"Oh yeah, Mr. Bible belt, what makes you so sure?"

Jay played a few more cards and nonchalantly responded, "'Cause I've seen 'em."

Now it was Earls turn to deadpan. "So demons aren't real because you've seen them?"

"Mm hmm."

"What the hell kind of logic is that?"

Jay put down his hand and gave his full attention to Earl. "Demon's ain't from hell. A demon is what happens when a man loses his soul and lets the space fill up with hate, and anger, and fear, and sadness, and lust. I've seen demons. This won' no demon." He lowered his gaze and returned to playing cards, albeit more sullen.

Losing interest in the show, Zack turned in his bean bag to face them. "So like, what did the tracks look like? You said they were all twisted and shit?"

Earl turned in his seat a little to face his way. "They looked like human hands, but wrong. Maybe it was how the mud slipped when it stepped, but the fingers seemed too thick, and the palm looked like it was too wide. And what the hell would someone be doing walking on their hands out here? I'm telling you, it's wrong. Unnatural. Unholy."

Zack scratched his head and thought for a minute. "What if it was, like, a gorilla or something? I mean I know chimps aren't huge, but they're *cut*. Yo, I saw this picture online of a chimp with no hair, that thing looked like a bodybuilder. So, like, what if a gorilla got out of a zoo?"

Earl waved a hand dismissively. "Skinny, where the hell is there a zoo near here?"

"Well, like, you know those stories about dogs runnin' for a stupid long ways to get back to their owners, or birds, and whales, and turtles, and shit that migrate all over the world? It could have ran super far."

Tim, without looking up from his book, simply chimed in, "Aliens."

Caught off guard, Jay just started laughing at the absurdity of the statement, then started to laugh more at how sure of himself he sounded. "Tim, brother, I really don't think aliens came down to play with our axes when we ain't lookin'."

Still reading his book Tim said, "All I'm saying is, I saw shit in the desert that I can't explain."

Jay thought for a moment. "There might be somethin' to that gorilla thing, actually. What's that old sayin'? Someone's razor? The simple answer is the right one, usually."

Earl put his hands up, bowing out of the conversation, but not before adding, "Demons, I'm telling you."

They laid the topic to rest for the night while the show went on in the background. They half watched the showmen craft their robots, but they all perked up when the fight was about to start.

Zack leaned back in his seat so he could look down the bus and shout, "Hey, old man, get ready to pay up, they're about to throw down!"

With a throaty grunt, Tim set down his book, stood up, and sauntered over. As he passed behind Zack he tousled his braided hair and said, "In your dreams, Skinny."

Zack swatted the hand away and shot a glare at Tim. Then smiled and settled back into his bean bag.

The mechanics were performing their final strength tests, but the croc bot hadn't had enough reinforcement along its jaw. The snapping of the weld was punctuated by an appropriately dramatic musical sting. The collective groans of disappointment filled the bus, with the exception of a loud whooping from Zack.

"Hell yeah! Pay up, old man. Shark is O.P!"

Tim rolled his eyes and clapped Zack on the shoulder. "Keep your britches on, if you've got enough ass to keep them up. Show's not over yet."

In lieu of a robot death battle, the show brought in two animal experts and overlaid their description of a fight with a computer animated battle between a great white and a saltwater croc.

The whole thing was very anticlimactic and ended with, "-*and once the crocodile got a hold of the shark it would perform its signature move, the death roll. The only problem being, once both animals were upside down, their fatal flaws would reveal themselves. Both leviathans are unable to move. When on their backs they are effectively paralyzed, but the shark has the advantage as they sink into the depths together. The shark doesn't need air. Once the prehistoric predator runs out of oxygen, it's game over.*"

Eleven: Close Encounters

It was the weekend, which meant the camp got to take it easy for a while. Everyone was eager to find a distraction. A lot had happened as of late and people were on edge. Some rest and relaxation was in order. Besides, the forecast called for rain again in the coming week, but for now the sun was back and it felt good to bask in its rays.

Jay stepped out of the bus and took in the fresh mid-morning air. He was feeling especially good today for some reason. The sun had just come up, but the day was already warming. He looked around and saw some of the guys raking and shoveling a large square of dirt. He decided to investigate and called out, "What yall doin'? You're a touch early for fall. Ain't no leaves to rake yet."

Alejandro looked up and tossed the shovel full of debris out of the square. "Sup, J-man. I know it ain't no damn fall. We're clearing a spot for some volleyball Yo, you want in?"

Jay put his hands on his hips as he surveyed the field. After a moment he piped up and said, "No thanks, there's only room 'nough for one sport in my heart."

"Oh yeah, cowboy? Let me guess, you only watch Sunday night 'foo'bah'. Watch them big men score the touch point."

"Nah, mine is the game of games; the game of kings." He looked Alejandro dead in the eye and with an impish grin said, "Curling."

Between his frustrated laughing Alejandro was able to shout out, "Get the fuck out of here."

With his head held high, Jay marched off to find someone else to harass. He quickly found his next victim in Tim, who had his head buried under the hood of a backhoe. It had been giving them trouble lately and Tim was the resident Mr. Fix-it.

Silently as a cat, Jay crept up behind Tim, who was engrossed in his work as he tried to leverage a nut off of a panel. Jay slammed his palms into the metal frame with a mighty crash as he yelled, "Wake up!"

For his trouble, Jay nearly caught a wrench with his teeth. The old man was *much* faster when he was scared.

"For the love of- if you ever scare me like that again I'm going to literally bury you, child." For emphasis Tim slammed the wrench against the backhoe. Returning to the stuck nut, he leveraged it off in one twist with his angry old man strength.

With a nervous smile Jay said, "I hear 'ya." He took a moment and looked at the great machine, considering it. "So, can you really fix this thing?"

Tim grumpily turned back to his work, brow furrowed. "If I got the right parts and tools. I got more than enough know-how."

"Is there anything here you *can't* fix?"

"Nope. I've got a lifetime of vehicular work under my belt. There's barely a thing on this earth I haven't worked on at one time or another."

Intrigued, Jay took up the challenge and threw out a guess. "Car engines?"

"Oh please, I cut my teeth on car engines. Do better."

"Boats."

"I had a buddy a while back who I'd go fishing with. I fixed that oversized POS more times than I can count."

"Huh." Jay thought for a moment, running through vehicles. "How about a plane?"

"Single engine crop duster. Called her Beulah."

"Ok, smart guy, I got one for 'ya. A tank."

Tim cackled while he tinkered with the backhoe. "M1A2 Abrams Main Battle Tank."

"What? You did not work on no tank, old man."

With another cackle Tim put the cover back on and leaned against the tread of the hoe while he wiped his hands off with an oily rag. "Sure did. Abrams, couple of different types of troop transports, Humvees. Even had the privilege of helping on a chinook repair job."

Jay gave a long, impressed whistle, then a thought hit him. "A hovercraft!"

"A hovercraft?"

"Yeah, you know, one of those big bastards, blows air down real hard so it hovers off the ground. You ever work on one 'a them?"

"Now where the hell am I going to get my hands on a damn hovercraft? Kids these days and their crazy space toys. 'Hovercraft', psh. Army don't use no damn hovercraft."

They laughed for a bit and Jay took up leaning on the tread himself. It was ridiculously uncomfortable so he settled for sitting on it instead. They stared off, looking over the mountains and trees for several peaceful moments before Jay nudged him with his foot. "You served?"

Tim didn't answer immediately, but after a few minutes he crackled out a simple, "Yeah."

"Y'ever go on deployment?"

Again, Tim didn't answer right away. "Afghanistan. I was out there scraping sand out of the oil and engines."

There was a long pause in the conversation. Suddenly the mood didn't seem quite so peaceful. He wanted to keep asking questions, but Tim didn't seem like he was willing to share much. While he was thinking about something he could ask that wouldn't end horrible, Tim broke the thought.

"Kid. I can feel those gears turning. I know you're no stranger to the shit this world can throw at you, but sometimes you see some shit that just cuts you down so low you'll never rise back up; not the same as before. And it's real easy to stray from the path when you roll into a ditch that deep." He rolled his sleeve up higher until it was above his elbow, exposing his arm. It was covered in track marks. "You would not *believe* how cheap it is over there. And if you find something that keeps you from waking up screaming or thinking about how to kill your own guys, you fucking take that shit, but there's no way you can hide something like that forever." Tim paused and gazed into the world with a thousand-yard stare, retreating into his memories. "It was the laughing. That's what pushed me over the edge. They were laughing about it."

Tim gave a long sigh as he rubbed his eyes and shook his head, talking more to himself than anybody else, "But that's not here, I'm not there, I'm off the streets, I have a job now, out in nature. There's life all around me and I'm fine."

Jay reached out and firmly patted him on the shoulder before letting his hand rest there and giving him a good squeeze. "I'm glad you're here, brother. You're a better man than most."

With a sniff Tim cleared his throat, which sounded like rocks in a blender. He patted the hand on his shoulder before shrugging it off and returning to his surly self. "Ah, what do you know. Now **get**. I'm busy playing with my toys."

Jay hopped down from the massive tread and patted the dirt from his seat. "See you later, old man."

"I thought I told you to get lost. Kids these days; never listening to their elders."

Jay wandered around aimlessly for a bit until he found himself on the edge of camp looking for scraps of wood he could use to whittle into animals; or maybe a good, strong walking stick. He could carve the head of it to have a cougar head or something. Hell, if he got good enough maybe he could sell them when he got back to town.

A branch snapped loudly off in the distance and when he looked up he saw Pharrell looking around cautiously before making a beeline for the trees. Jay knew that look. What the sam hell was that man up to? Probably something damn foolish.

Shaking his head, he stomped off after him. He wasn't hard to follow. Every now and again he'd hear a crash or a snap up ahead

100

and follow after it until he caught a flash of red flannel about thirty feet forward.

"Pharrell," he called out as he picked up the pace, trying to catch up, "will you just wait a cotton pickin' minute?"

Pharrell stopped in his tracks and slowly turned. "*Excuse me?*"

As he caught up Jay tried to puzzle out what his problem was, then he realized the implication. "Ah, yeah, southern expression... poor choice of words. I know why you're out here, but why the hell are you out here *alone?*"

"Because no one else is looking, and no one will help me. I asked Mat if we could get a search party together, and he gives me a bunch of bull shit about how we're too remote and he's a low priority because we don't 'know for certain' that he's in danger. Like *hell* we don't know he's in danger. And nobody else will help me, either. I asked everyone I thought would even consider. So here I am. Alone."

Jay could see the shimmer in his eyes and hear the quiver of that last word; 'alone'. He stared into those puppy dog eyes, that determined face and he couldn't help but respect the loyalty. Plus, if he was being honest, Mclean's disappearance had unsettled him more than he cared to show.

"Ok," he said with a sigh, "what's the plan?"

Pharrell looked him up and down before asking incredulously, "Seriously? You? You're going to help me look for him?"

"The hell's that supposed to mean?"

"It means there's a reason I didn't ask you. You probably hated him more than anybody, besides Tim. Why the hell would you help get him back?"

That gave Jay a pause. He thought on it for a moment before answering. "Sure, I think he's a dangerous ass hat who deserves to get knocked down every last peg, but for reasons that will forever elude me, he's your friend, and... you're *my* friend. Sometimes, friends are all we got."

"This isn't like helping me move a damn couch, Jay."

There was so much more he wanted to say, but there was a time and a place for everything and this wasn't it. "Look, I'm literally the only person in the world who's goin' to help you right now, so either I'm goin' out to help you, or I'm goin' back and tellin' Mat you're out here alone."

Pharrell had to give him another look up and down, trying to gleam some level of insight, but when he looked into Jay's eyes he saw the same determination that he felt himself, even if he didn't understand why it was there. "Fine, whatever. Let's just keep going."

They traveled in silence for a long while. The sun moved across the sky, but in the dense foliage of the trees, they barely noticed. The day was hot and in the small patches where it pierced the green ceiling above them they could see the ripples and waves of the air, and feel the intensity of the radiation. Here in the deep woods and shade, though, the air was cool; especially as they dipped into the valleys where water trickled down in clear streams. As they descended, they could feel the temperature drop significantly more until the chill almost made their sweat soaked bodies shiver.

The dirt beneath their feet was still moist and soft from the millions of pine needles, all burying the layer beneath. With each step the smell of fresh earth was kicked up, perfuming the air with the richest scents of nature.

It was so still, this deep in. From each direction a new sound met their ears, bathing the whole environment in a serene beauty. From off in the distance the quick drumming of a woodpecker would echo off the trees. A sudden rustling in the vines and shrubs would produce a squirrel, or a rabbit darting away as it realized something larger was tromping by. Bird songs and the occasional snapping of a branch off in the distance were the sounds of the day.

Their only contribution to the noise besides their foot fall was the occasional shout of, "Charles", or "Charlie", called without reply.

Some hours passed by and they found themselves at an open field of wild grass at the edge of the forest. A clear trench had recently been pushed through the tall grass that led to a boulder field at the far side. The stony meadow was slightly higher than the grass field, and the whole area beyond was littered with gravel, brush weeds and the occasional struggling pine that had managed to survive in the tough soil. The only other decoration to the rough landscape were boulders; stones ranging in size from a simple chair to an entire house.

Panting heavily from the brisk hike, Pharrell wiped the sweat from his face. "This is it. This is where Earl said he lost the trail. We'll start here and see if we can find anything; any sign of him."

Jay copied the motion and pushed the sweat through the short bristles of his hair and scratched the sweat droplets from his growing beard. "Listen, I don't want to bring you down, but 'any sign of him' could mean, well, it could mean more of a *final* conclusion than you're hopin' for."

"No. No, he's alive. I can feel it. I know he is. He's out here, somewhere. We just have to find him."

Behind Pharrell's back, Jay rolled his eyes, not wanting to expend the energy arguing. "Ok then, how's this for a plan? We split up and every ten seconds or so we call out for Mclean. That way we can cover more ground, keep tabs on where the other one is and if he's nearby, he'll hear us. Also, let's use his last name. I think you were the only one who called him anything else. If he ain't right minded he might respond better to Mclean."

With a nod, Pharrell turned into the ruff hillside and began yelling at the top of his lungs, "Mclean!" His voice echoed off the smooth faces of the stones, calling out quieter and quieter as the shout dwindled into nothingness.

With that, the search began in earnest. Jay felt a second wind go through him, prompted by the gusto Pharrell took to the task. The second wind was short lived however, as the sun beat down upon them mercilessly. Sweat poured from their brows, and it was only now, in the unrelenting bombardment of heat that Jay realized his incredible thirst. His tongue was rough against his teeth, what little spit he had felt as thick as honey and as sour as old milk. He wanted nothing more than to dive into a cool mountain river and drink deeply in the freshwater, but that was just a fantasy, he had to keep his head in the game; the excruciatingly hot, dry game.

The rocks echoed with the shouts for "Mclean, Mclean", but there was never a reply. Jay was tired, hungry and dangerously dehydrated. Plus, he realized, significantly far from camp. In a bid to get out of the sun for a moment, he chose to investigate some little trees that were barely bigger than a man, but they gave enough shade to at least take a moment for himself. He struggled to push by some tough, low tree branches, trying to wrestle his way between the stout pines. Then his grip slipped and it punched him hard in the face. With a groan he stood up and tasted blood on his already swelling lip. A white hot flash of anger beat out all rational thought. He roared and threw all his weight on the limb until it snapped, causing him to crash to the dusty ground.

Choking on dust and spitting dirt and blood, he saw it. "Phar- Pharreh- Pharrell," he coughed, "Pharrell, come 'ear."

There was the sound of hurried feet and the shifting of rocks, dirt, and gravel as his friend came rushing over. "What? What is it? Did you find him?"

"Sorta."

The pair found themselves looking out over a large, flat topped boulder. It looked like a giant, natural table, long enough to seat a dozen people. Littered on top of the table were clothes. Mclean's clothes, by the look of it. The pants and underwear were huge and there were his socks and the sleeveless shirt he was wearing the night he stormed off. His boots, however, were nowhere to be seen. The pants and shirt were laying on the rock like someone had lifted him straight up and the clothes just fell off him into a pile. The socks were farther away, like he took one off, dropped it, took a step and removed the other.

Pharrell's expression was panicked. He dashed onto the boulder and began meticulously pouring over the clothes, looking at each one in turn, closely and hurriedly, looking for anything that might explain what happened.

He looked up at Jay with a cocktail of emotions. "I don't understand. There's no cuts, no tears, no blood, nothing. Why would he just, why would he do this? Any of this?"

He fell to his knees as he became overwhelmed with emotion and silently cried, tears dropping from his cheeks, his mind whirling as it tried to find an answer, an explanation to this madness.

All Jay could do was walk over, plop himself down on the overly hot rock and just sit in silence with his friend. They sat; neither of them knew for how long, just trying to think of what to do next. After some time, Pharrell had dried his tears and simply sat with a thousand yard stare, looking at the clothes for a long, long time; until something broke the silence.

"Mac Clean!" came a strange, harsh, husky voice.

Both men leapt to their feet. They both knew what Mclean sounded like. His voice boomed like thunder and rang with confidence. This was not that voice. This voice was raspy and unsure. Like speaking new words in a foreign tongue. It almost seemed to be tasting the word instead of speaking it.

"Mac Clean," it called again. The horrid voice echoed off the rocks, bouncing all around them, concealing from what direction it was sourced. Of the words that were spoken, the emphasis was wrong. The "L" was too heavy. So much about the spoken word was illicit.

They looked at each other, both were equally unsure of what was happening or what to do, so they paused. They waited. They listened. The world was silent, now. Not even the animals dared to speak.

Then, all around them came another, preternatural call, "Jchar Leee!"

They could feel the blood drain from their faces. The primal urge to flee had viciously clawed its way to the front of their minds. That was it. That was the final straw. They both shot off the rock and without a word started sprinting toward the edge of the boulder field. The heat, forgotten. Their thirst, bygone. They were overcome by such terror that all rational thought vacated their minds. With such primal instincts driving them, the conscious mind had no room or control. Time had no meaning. Total exhaustion was but a fleeting nuisance in the face of the fright that overtook them. With each step their minds imagined the unknown "It" behind them, the unseen Snag that could claim them without warning. The thing was always just one more powerful, predatory leap away in their minds, before it would catch them and make them disappear, just like Mclean.

Eventually, two sweaty and wide eyed men broke through the tree line of the camp, and didn't stop running until they reached the safety of the busses. Gasping like fish out of water, they collapsed to the ground, both their eyes glued to the forest they had just escaped.

Pharrell managed to tear his gaze from the woods and whirled towards Jay. "What," he gasped, "was that?"

Still trying to catch his breath, all he could do was shake his head. A long line of thin drool spooling from his lower lip. He didn't care. He was alive, but there was someone in those woods. They both heard it. He wasn't crazy. Pharrell ran just like he did! "Let's," he had to swallow to try and wet his throat, "we need to tell Mat." He said, finally deciding to wipe the drool from his face.

Pharrell nodded, vigorously. Slowly, he got his breathing under control. "Water?"

Jay nodded in turn. "Yeah, first water. I think I'm *actually* dyin'."

Mat folded his arms and leaned back in his office chair. "So you, the both of you, *definitely* heard someone out there calling for Mclean?"

Jay leaned forward, gesturing wildly as he spoke. "Yeah, but it was all kinds a wrong sound'n. Now I'm serious, Mat, we heard it, and it turned us as yellow as mustard! We couldn't *get* out of there fast enough. We was talkin' after, and we think we've got an idea. You ever hear 'bout that gorilla they taught to speak? An escaped gorilla or somethin' seems like maybe what we got here. What if it heard us a-hollerin' and learned to, I don't know, mimic us or somethin'?"

Mat shook his head slowly. "I don't think so. That gorilla learned sign language. Their throat plumbing is all wrong for talking, *but*... and as crazy as it sounds, some kind of loose ape does fit pretty well. If it belongs to some hobunk hermit who wants us gone, that could explain why it's out here in the first place. The exotic pet trade is big business."

Pharrell interjected, waving his hands just as wildly as Jay. "And what about the clothes? Why the hell would he just take them off?"

All Mat could do was shrug. "Really anything we can say at this point would be speculation, but I'd guess a mild case of hypothermia. It was night when he left and after hiking that far he was definitely sweating. One of the final stages makes you feel hot and it makes people take their clothes off. It's not uncommon. But...," a thought seemed to enter his head and he took a moment to mull it over, "the man that went missing back in town, they found his clothes too, and they think he disappeared during the day..."

They all looked at each other in silence until Pharrell spoke up. "So, what does that mean?"

Again, all Mat could do was shrug and shake his head. "I have no god damn idea, but I have a bad feeling about all this."

The three of them sat in silence, thinking, no one wanting to be the one to say it. The stillness of the small office was suffocating and seemed to hang eternally.

Finally Mat spoke, which seemed to start the world turning again. "Pharrell, we're going to move you into bus eighteen, they have a free bunk. With everything going on we can't have people alone at any time. I'm doubling down on the buddy system, too. Work, shits, showers, I don't care; you have someone near you at all times. I'll make the announcement tonight."

* * * * * * * * *

The Night Sun was bright. It would get brighter. It had to be careful. The Blooded One and The Solitary came this way. It knew The Blooded One, It remembered the smell of its blood, its sweat, its fear. The Solitary was new. It didn't have the smells of others on it. The Solitary was alone. Easy meat.

It watched as the last Small Sun darkened in the territory of the loud Tall Ones. They were strange, the Small Suns, made of Not-Fire. It knew Fire, It hated Fire. The Tall Ones from long ago would use it. The sky would sometimes explode and fire would slice down in a flash of light, or a piece of the sky would fall, burn and start a Fire that ate many Trees. It hated Fire more than Pack Jaws. It tried to ignore the thoughts, It had better things to do.

It had learned much during its time in their territory. They had fine stone tools, better than Its own. They had water that was hard and as sharp as any knife. They had food in their strange little caves, their dens. Their tools were dangerous, though. They screamed in ways that hurt the ear. It would not take those tools when they died. It would take more of the hard, smooth stone ones that shined. It liked their shine; and their weight.

For now, it would wait here. Wait for them to sleep. Only when It was sure the Tall Ones were sleeping would It risk being in the light of the Night Sun.

Twelve: The Mountains Maw

Morning came and the men roused themselves from the comfort of their warm beds. With heavy hands they lifted their heavy boots and slid their feet into the leather bricks. Then with heavy footsteps they walked out into the cold morning air. It wasn't arctic cold by any means, but it was chilly enough to see their breath fog the air. Maybe that was why, that morning, it was so hard to see. All the animals in all the woods, breathing and adding their breaths together. Low clouds had rolled in overnight, giving the world a misty blanket that curled around the grass and blurred the tops of the trees making them appear like they reached up endlessly into the sky.

Jay hoped it would warm up and the fog would clear, but the regional forecast said there was going to be a lot of wet and cold weather headed their way for a few days. He looked out toward his favorite view, the strip of trees they had cut to make the road. It let him see the mountains far off in the distance, and the mountains behind them, and the mountains behind *them*, and the mountains so far away that they blurred into the skyline. Today they were gone. All of them. The world ended just a few hundred feet in every direction. Ended in a wall of imposing, diffuse white-grey.

Farther down the row of busses came a shout. "Mat! Mat, come here!"

Mat had been standing outside of his trailer door, nursing a steaming hot cup of coffee with both hands wrapped around the mug. He set it down in the doorway and ran to the call. A small crowd had wandered over to see the commotion. They parted to let their boss through until he was able to get to the front door of the newly emptied bus number twenty-three. The front door had been left unlocked overnight, and with the morning, it was discovered to have been left ajar, but what immediately snagged Mat's attention was the first step leading into the bus. For on the first step was a dirty, mud caked print; not of a foot, but of a hand.

He turned his attention to the one who had called him. "Kevin, you found it like this?"

109

The scrawny, young blond nodded. "Yeah, I stepped out, saw it was open, so I went to close it up. Then I saw *that* shit."

"Ok, everybody stays here."

He placed his foot on the step and slowly, silently poked his head inside. His unscrupulous gaze dissected every inch of the interior, looking for the slightest hint that the bus was still occupied. Satisfied that there was nothing lurking in the corners, he stepped in. The place was a mess. Before it had only housed Pharrell and Mclean, so there wasn't an overabundance of possessions. Moving Pharrell to another bus had further reduced the occupancy, but for how little there was inside, the interior had been thoroughly trashed.

What little furniture there was, was knocked over, the bed sheets on all four beds were gone, and the mattresses were disheveled. Every cabinet was left open, and two of them even had their doors ripped off their hinges. There was a broken lightbulb, its shards littering the carpet. Dirt was everywhere and on everything, ground into the fabrics where the intruder had stepped. The emergency back door had been left open as well.

Mat jumped out the back and followed the tracks that lead away from the bus. He followed them all the way to bus number eighteen. Pharrell was standing in the doorway of his bus, a look of shock and deeply disturbed horror on his face. Mat looked at him and said, "It looks like you've made a friend..."

Pharrell nodded, wide eyed and a bit stunned. "I think the move was a good call, boss."

"I don't suppose you heard anything last night?"

Pharrell just shook his head while he looked, transfixed at the tracks at his feet.

With a deep breath Mat rubbed his face and groaned, weighing his deeply unpleasant options. After several moments he came to a decision and stepped out so everyone could hear him as he shouted, "Ok, everyone, I don't pretend to know what's happening around here, but we've got a man missing and it looks like they tried to get another one of us last night. I know we just

110

went over the doubled-up buddy system, so I won't waste your time, but I can *NOT* stress its importance enough. Now I'll be joining you out in the field today and I will be bringing the rifle. If you even *suspect* something is off, you radio me. I've already contacted the authorities, but due to the circumstances, they gave me the runaround about how they can't come out unless there's been a crime. Tonight, I *WILL* be contacting the authorities again and demanding a force come out here to investigate, so if you think something is evidence, keep your hands off of it, and radio me. Now, let's get out there."

Afterward, everyone found their positions, put their nose to the grindstone and worked, but everyone kept their guard up. No one could really hear because of the noise, but everyone kept their head on a swivel. They worked slower than they usually did, but they knew what was at stake so the decline in productivity was overlooked.

Jay was doing his usual thing, falling trees, cutting notches, watching for snags, not being kidnapped by a crazed murder-gorilla. During one of his many glances up, he saw Tim driving the harvester wearing the biggest damn smile he'd ever seen plastered on his leathery face as he rumbled by. At least someone was having fun during all this. Jay couldn't forget the events of the day before. He kept hearing the voice calling out to them. It was like it was from nowhere and everywhere all at once. Just thinking about the pale imitation of speech made his skin crawl. Then there were the tracks in their camp. Whatever was out there knew where they slept. Had he and Pharrell brought it back with them? He shook his head, trying to kick the thoughts out of his mind. Visually sweeping his surroundings again didn't disparage the paranoia that held on so tightly to him.

The fog hadn't let up even a little, either. In fact, now that he looked at it he was pretty sure it had gotten thicker. He was about to get back to work when his radio keyed.

"Hey, this is Black George over at the northern site, does anyone have eyes on Alejandro?"

A slow trickle of responses all replying "negative" flowed over the radio until Mat's voice came through. "Copy that, George. Jay and Pharrell, you're near the north site, right? Find George and I'll meet you up there in a minute."

Jay propped up his chainsaw against a tree and laid the heavy shoulder belt next to it. "Copy that. See you soon."

It took a few minutes to hike up the hill and up the dirt road they'd made to the north site, but they hiked it and arrived about the same time as Mat, who had jogged up, rifle slung on his shoulder by its strap. George was sitting on a stump and stood up as they approached.

Mat greeted him with a nod and immediately asked, "Ok, what happened?"

George always moved quite a bit when he talked, and it always made Jay a little uncomfortable for some reason. Maybe because it was too hard to focus on one spot and that was how you got stabbed. Forgoing the thought, he engaged in the present moment.

George waved a hand in the direction he had been walking. "I don't know, one second he's right behind me and then the mother fucker's just like 'Peace'."

Nodding, Mat analyzed the situation. "How far behind you was he?"

"Shit, I don't know, thirty feet or some shit. Dude was *right* behind me."

"And you radioed the second you noticed he was gone?"

"Well, like, I looked for him all around me and back the way we came; but yeah, as soon as I saw he was gone I was like, 'anybody got eyes'?"

Again, Mat nodded. "Ok, if you two were heading east and there's workers to the south, he could only have gone north or

112

west. George, you're with me, we'll backtrack and see if he didn't just go back. Pharrell, Jay, you two head north. If anybody spots him, you radio me. I don't like this. Let's move, and stay safe."

George and Mat took off at a brisk pace down the path of mud and quickly vanished into the pea soup fog. Jay and Pharrell cut north and a little west to make up for not knowing how far back Alejandro disappeared. They broke up like they did for the search for Mclean, far enough to cover ground, close enough to call and react.

Concern germinated in Jay's mind, and it soon grew into panic. They crawled over the steep embankments and wove around trees looking for tracks, clothes, gear, anything that would tell them where he had gone. They alternated calling his name, over and over, but never a reply came.

The whole nature of the situation made him uneasy. His stomach felt heavy and he was overcome with the frantic urge to run; whether towards, or away from here, he didn't know. He felt as helpless as a man in the ocean, knowing there are beasts deep down, lurking right on the edge of light, waiting for their chance to surge up and drag him down.

The frenzied search felt like it had gone on for hours, but he knew it could only have been about thirty minutes. His heart was racing, sweat beaded on his forehead and dripped to his nose, not helped in the slightest by the humidity.

Then, thankfully, Pharrell came over the radio. "Mat, I found him. He's by the cluster of cedar we scouted last week, walking north through the field."

The radio crackled back, "Keep eyes on him, do not approach until I get there."

With a second wind and fueled by hope, Jay sprinted toward Pharrell. He knew, generally, where he was from the calling before, and it only took a moment for Jay to spot him. He put his hands to his mouth and was about to call out when Pharrell furiously motioned him down and pointed.

Turning to follow his finger, Jay spied Alejandro, but something about him was off. He was walking through the grass in a clearing, his form barely more than a specter in the mist, but it was him, no doubt. What was so clearly off about him was his gait. The man didn't walk like a man. He shuffled lazily, shambling slowly forward like the undead or a man deprived of rest. His arms swayed loosely at his side and his feet left drag marks, bending the blades of grass along his path. Jay was sure he'd stumble if the terrain became even slightly uneven. But perhaps the most peculiar element of the whole amble was his head, which never tilted, bent or swayed. Instead, it seemed to be perfectly set, focused on a single point that no amount of lethargic shambling could dissuade.

Jay had never seen him like this, like a staggering drunk with the focus of a sharpshooter. Since Alejandro was already at the edge of his misty vision, he steeled himself and decided that he had to know more; and like Mat said, 'keep eyes on him', so he was really just following orders. Jay crouched down and began awkwardly running into the field, his knees thudding against his chest with each step. He moved as silently as he could, considering his thick clothes and heavy boots. He crept further into the field until he could see across to the trees on the other side.

Then, through the haze, he saw something. At least he thought he did. It was like he was seeing something out of the corner of his eye, only the haze was directly in front of him. It looked spherical, at least that was the impression it left; and it seemed to glow a faint yellow. The disk hovered in the tree line about eight feet off the ground and as it hung, suspended in midair by unseen forces, it seemed to thrum and pulse with a pleasant evenness that made his eyes feel heavy, his knees feel weak, and the base of his neck to be soothed with warmth.

Feeling the strangeness scratching at his mind, he shook his head and dislodged the mild sensations, but Alejandro gazed directly into the orb and was completely enthralled. As Jay continued to creep closer he began to make out the form of something beneath the globe. The form was shrouded in mist and concealed by foliage, but there was definitely a darkened shape in the woods. Whatever was there, it seemed to be calling their friend to an unknown, but doubtlessly horrible fate.

There was a crashing sound behind him, far off into the mists. He turned to see Mat charging down a slope with reckless abandon. He stopped near Pharrell and the two exchanged words before Pharrell pointed to the two men in the field. Mat looked out and met Jay's gaze. Jay lifted his hand and pointed to the figure hidden in the wilderness, then mimed holding a rifle, complete with kick back.

The clumsy message must have been clear enough, because immediately the rifle snapped up and was shouldered into Mat's firm frame. He followed the psychic line drawn out by Jay and fired into the woods.

In the next instant, the world seemed to tear at the seams as a pain stabbed his mind like a railroad spike had driven into his skull by a ten-ton hammer. The instant after, the pain vanished like it had never been, but the flash burn of tortuous agony caused him to plummet into the ground and clutch his head in his hands. Jay's lungs refused to fill as he choked and gasped for air, his throat locked, and his eyes blurring with tears.

Then he found his voice and a hallowed scream slowly grew from him until it was a frenzied, manic bellow that squeezed his lungs and could fray the very strings that bound the soul. Jay didn't even know why he was screaming, but it was the only course left to his wounded mind. He laid in the grass and mud, doubled over from the shock and shaking like he was suffering from fever.

He could hear voices. They were close, but sounded so far away. Any meaning that they babbled was lost as he fought back sickness that threatened to expel his breakfast. Eventually he started to regain control of his faculties and could take stock of what was going on around him. Mat and Pharrell were over him, asking if he was ok, yelling his name.

On a trembling arm he tried to prop himself up. It took more than a single attempt, but he managed it while his vision fluctuated in and out of focus. Several times he had to wipe away tears that welled up and threatened to take his sight. George was with Alejandro, who was on all fours and puking his guts out. All George could do was pat his friend on the back and hold his long, black hair out of his face.

Jay fully righted himself and hugged his knees. There was a tightness in his abdomen, and it hurt like he'd been punched in the gut. His body didn't know which it wanted to do more, puke or shit itself. It took every ounce of his focus to keep it from doing both. He managed to regain control of his insides and groaned, "What happened?"

Mat stole a look around before answering. "I have no god damn idea. I took a warning shot and then me and Pharrell and George got stabbed with a migraine straight out of hell, but you and Ali went down hard. You were screaming, and honestly, I thought I had hit you somehow."

"So you felt it too? I thought I'd seen someone with a flashlight or a lantern or somethin'. I think it was makin' him all confrazzled."

With a grunt, Mat stood up. "I heard some crashing in the woods over there. Pharrell, you stay with him, I'm going to take a look."

With his trademarked, heart melting, puppy dog eyes Pharrell looked to Jay. "Are you doing ok? What in the hell happened?"

Shaking less now, Jay replied, "I don't know. After the shot, it felt like my head was gettin' split'n two. How's he doin'," he said with a nod toward the other two.

George looked up and gave them a thumbs up just as Alejandro gave another dry heave. "We all good here. Hey, the fuck you see out there?"

"I, I don't know. There was a light, like maybe a lantern or a flashlight. Then just below it there was, somebody, I think."

Everyone took a few moments to rest. Their reprieve was, unfortunately, cut short as Mat returned, tromping over with the rifle in hand.

"I found a blood trail and some more of those gorilla tracks. Gentlemen, let's get to the bottom of this."

—————————

After some quick radio chatter and some not so quick descending a tree, Earl met up with the group. Tim and Jay had volunteered to help track. Jay was allowed to come because he had come the closest to seeing the mysterious figure and could possibly identify them. Tim had combat training. Earl was *volun-told* because of his tracking abilities and Pharrell wasn't taking no for an answer. So the five of them grouped up and started the hunt.

Earl was up front, following the slowly dwindling blood trail. As the blood thinned, he began to rely more on prints and paths. Tim was on point with Earl so that at least one of them had eyes up and looking for danger. The other three marched behind in a triangle formation. Mat in the front with the rifle, Jay and Pharrell in the back keeping eyes up to their respective sides and behind.

The formation marched on, ever alert, ready to react on a hair trigger. Their ears scraped up every little sound the forest made, their eyes peeled back the foliage to suss out any secret's that might be concealed. It was exhausting, not only the long march through the primal lands, but the constant hyper alertness paid to every cluster of leaves and every branch, picking it apart visually to make sure nothing was going to leap out and get them. The situation was life or death and the slightest misstep could end them.

It was, admittedly, made easier with five people covering one another. The blood had stopped long ago and now they followed the prints alone. It was easy where the earth was soft or the forest floor had been lifted as it kicked off, but it was more difficult around hard ground where they would have to look for other signs like broken foliage, tree limbs or just fan out and search for where the trail picked up. The sun was well overhead now and they had been steadily going uphill for the past half hour or more.

Exhausted, the group decided to take shelter in the shadow of a large boulder. Earl stood panting and took a cloth from his pocket to wipe the ocean of sweat from his face and head. The fog had broken as the day heated up and although the sun was behind a sheet of grey clouds, it was still warm in the midday.

After a moment, Earl spoke up. "So," he said as he caught his breath, "my guess is you grazed it, because it stopped bleeding even though it kept moving. I'd bet good money that right now it's going somewhere it feels safe so it can lick its wounds."

Mat was breathing hard too, but he was still going strong. "Well it doesn't seem to have slowed it down. Or them. We still don't know what we're dealing with; not for sure."

Wiping his sweaty face on his cloth again, Earl shook his head. "It wouldn't slow down, not at first. With all that adrenaline it wouldn't have even felt that it got shot for a while."

Tim had scouted ahead a few hundred feet and came sneaking back. Out of everyone, he seemed to be the least winded and was still chugging. "I couldn't find tracks, but there's a cave or something up ahead, hidden under an old tree."

They all looked at each other in turn before looking expectantly at Earl. "Uh, yeah, a cave could be a place where it could feel safe."

Swinging the gun into a comfortable grip Mat spoke up. "Ok, before we think of any kind of plan, does anyone have any light on them?"

Tim reached into his pocket and pulled out a small pocket flashlight. "It's not much, but it's light."

Earl produced a lighter from his own pocket. "It's even less, but it's light. Although... Give me a minute."

Due to the excessive heat, Earl had taken off an outer layer of his work clothes long ago and tied it around his waist. He withdrew the garment and began tearing it into strips until the shirt was in tatters. Then he slid his work hatchet from its sheath on his belt and gathered up some sticks. He found some sturdy greenwood and split one end into quarters. He slid smaller sticks down into the quartered end so the four prongs were held open. Then, with surprising nimbleness, he hauled himself up into a good strong spruce. After a moment he found a large clump of sap that oozed from the trunk and gathered it on the cloth strips. Once he was down, he rubbed each strip with the sap until they were stiff with

118

the gooey nectar. The stiff wraps were bound around a sizable pinecone and lowered into the prongs. Once the smaller sticks were removed, the prongs gripped the sappy cone tight. When the flame of the lighter licked the bundle, it erupted into a torrent of guzzling flames.

Holding his creation up for all to see, he proudly proclaimed, "I am man, and I control fire!"

Mat laughed through his nose and rolled his eyes. "Yeah, yeah, master of nature. How long will that thing last?"

"Twenty to thirty minutes. What's the plan, boss?"

"Tim will go first with the light, I'll go behind him with the rifle, you three-"

Tim cut him off abruptly with an agitated, "What? You want to run that line up by me again? 'Cause I thought I heard you say you're putting someone *in front* of the gun."

Mat cleared his throat uncomfortably before picking back up. "I'll go first with the rifle. Tim will go behind me and shine the light forward. Earl, you're behind him with the torch for radial light. Pharrell and Jay, you're in the back making sure nothing comes up behind us. With the torch you should be able to see well enough. We're not going to risk ourselves unnecessarily. We'll poke our heads in, if we don't find anything quick, we go back to camp and get those god damned, stubborn-ass police, or rangers, or National Guard, *someone* up here to help us with this."

Jay chimed in and asked, "What if we find the gorilla?"

"We shoot it. It's a dangerous animal. End of story. If we find its owner, we give him one chance to surrender, or he goes too. We're dealing with an unstable person and I'm not taking chances any more than I have to. Are we clear?"

They all nodded in turn. With the utmost caution, they slowly approached the cave, taking care not to trip on the rocks or send them sailing down the path. The mouth of the cave sat beneath a weathered, long dead tree. Like a tortured guardian, the old gnarl held the ground firm and kept the mouth yawning. In life, its roots snaked out in search of sustenance. In death, its skeletal roots crept along the mouth of the cave and protruded from the dirt and rock, and inspired images of bent and twisted teeth.

The group entered past the sun hardened roots and cast their lights down the stony throat. Flames and beams of light illuminated the rough and jagged walls. As they walked into the dark, the temperature quickly cooled. Their sweat drenched clothing chilled them all the more with every step they took. Jay tried to resist, but a shiver clawed its way down his spine. It was quiet here, but this wasn't the pleasant kind of quiet that the forest offered, where the silence of the world can be appreciated. It was an oppressive, pressurized silence that bore down upon them and made them yearn for any sound beyond their own breath and boots. The kind where the air itself seemed to squeeze their head, and made their mind claw desperately at anything that might be sound, but there was nothing found. Only the odd scuff of a boot or the slip of a hand against stone.

Jay looked up at his companions, and in the total silence his whisper seemed as loud as thunder. "Mat, you doin' ok up there?"

His only response was a small hand signal that waved him off, presumably telling him to stay quiet. By the rise and fall of his shoulders, Jay could see that Mat was breathing hard, harder than when he was hiking the mountain. Mat was clearly nervous, but he was on task and managing his fear. At least, he was trying to.

The cave continued its spiraled path downward, drilling into the mountain depths. The party hurdled its dips and ledges, squeezed through its narrow passages and stalked through the open chasms. The deeper they delved, the heavier the rock roof above them felt. Jay had to fight off visions of it collapsing and sealing them away to slowly starve and suffocate in the cold and the dark.

They could not tell how long they had traveled, but after what felt like an eternity, the cave opened into a wide belly, of sorts. A much larger cavity where they could stand up straight, and wide enough they could spread their arms without brushing against the sides. It was deep, too, trailing back farther than the torchlight could illuminate. A sweep of the flashlight revealed a much smaller chamber off to the side with a low ceiling and a pool of fresh water.

From its ceiling, some unknown source fed the pool with a small dribble of water.

They quickly swept their light over the room, looking to reveal any lurking madman or monstrosity, but none were found. Instead, they saw a large, flat-topped rock that was naturally embedded in the floor. The stone table was messily adorned with an eclectic assortment of horrid things. Atop the earthen table rested a collection of human skulls, with all but one of them in poor condition. The last one was still fresh, albeit missing some teeth. The others were much older, aged and brittle, each one showing signs of trauma. A bashed skull, a fractured maxilla, and one who'd had the back of their head cracked open. Teeth and small bones littered the table, some of man, some of beast. Crude, fibrous string had been used to tie the small bones together into a hodgepodge of shapes that vaguely resembled a dream catcher or charm, though the craft was a perversion of the concept.

Scattered across the stone shelf was a collection of incredibly rough and crudely constructed clay bowls and pots. They looked like they hadn't even been fired. Some were filled with water, presumably from the pool in the corner, some were filled with blood. The contents of one, Jay didn't recognize, but after a sniff he suspected it was fat, though from what, he dared not guess. Next to them was an obsidian knife, knapped to an edge sharper than a steel razor. Around the knife were dark stains with a metallic smell. Small bits of air-dried meat lay basking over smooth stones, their moisture dripping down to grow the pools of dark stains beneath them.

More small, dry bones littered the Stone Age kitchen. Upon inspection, one of the bowls contained a mixture of sap and honey. A flat chip of wood rested half dipped into the concoction. Blood stained the exposed wood and some more seemed to have made its way into the bowl after application.

Further in, there was a dull colored pile of modern-day fabrics. The linens were quickly identified as an odd assortment of clothes of various sizes, but the majority of the nest consisted of the missing bed sheets from the looted bus. Everything was soiled from dirt and a pungent urine smell clung to them. Littered all around the

121

bed were scraps of shoes. Leather bits, small rubber chunks, rough patches of cloth, a small piece of shoelace. There was one giant boot that wasn't completely destroyed, and even it had clearly bore deep bite marks.

Farther back still, lay a refuse pile. Larger bones comprised the bulk of it; the rest consisted of broken pieces of pottery, unusable stone knives, smaller bones, small scraps of cloth, and a dozen other tidbits of random debris.

The smell of the large chamber was powerful. It was a blend of thick, musty smells like mold or mildew. Under that there was a pungent musk; a gamey animal scent that Jay couldn't quite place, but was unmistakable as a wild beast. The faint aroma of the fresh, clean water was almost lost under the overpowering smell of old dirt, urine and... something else.

Tim examined the trash pile, inspecting the knives. None were salvageable. He sifted through the garbage, but didn't find anything that caught his interest until he brushed aside a small collection of bones. Something in the bottom of the pile glinted in the dim light. Dusting it off a bit he found something that looked like the blade to a miniature sword or bizarre, micro combat knife.

It was a small piece of metal, only an inch or two long. He had trouble picking it up as the thing was impossibly smooth, completely without tarnish, despite the horrendous condition it was found in. Down the two sides were tiny little serrations that ran its length, and upon closer inspection the tip was hollow. He must have been holding it more tightly than he realized, because during his inspection he'd cut himself several times without even feeling it. The cuts were shallow, but the fresh nicks began to ooze blood. He discarded the dangerous little thing back into the pile. He was about to turn back, but something else caught his eye.

He moved bits of pottery and bone out of his way to reveal some small, oval shaped arrowheads. They were knapped stones, like the knives, but something about them stuck out to him. As he rolled it over in his hands, he glanced up. He shined the light upward onto the wall and with a raspy gasp he slowly called out, "Fellas, I'm not so sure it's a gorilla."

Mat and Pharrell were busy probing the cave while Earl and Jay came over to see what was happening. Both stared open mouthed at the wall. Earl held his torch high to illuminate the wall in full.

Jay was the first to speak. "What the hell is this?"

Across the wall, from end to end, was a painting. Hundreds of small pictographs consumed the entire canvas, haphazardly doodled in almost every available space. They showed herds of animals moving over rivers, through plains, and forests. There were busts of different wild beasts, most were recognizable, but others were strange and foreign, and others still, impossible. Enormous cats with teeth the length of a man's forearm, elephants covered in fur, small horses that were painted with such minute detail that even their toes were masterfully illustrated. There was a... something that looked like a camel with an elephant trunk, if the trunk was shortened to just a wiggly nose. There were eagles, fish, plants, trees, and more all drawn in spectacular detail, all illustrated with shading and simple colors.

They marveled at the scene for so long that they could begin to recognize landmarks dotted around the map. To Jay, one mountain stood out more than the others, though this depiction of it still had its pointed peak. The images were painted with coarse, rudimentary pigment. Black was most heavily used, but also rich with reds from clay, white from ash, and several shades of a warm brown mixed from other earthy sources.

Illustrated in the center of the diagram was a smaller mountain with more detail than the rest. At the top, near the peak, a trail of tiny, human handprints led to a lonely tree that marked a tunnel. The serpentine path fed into a chamber at the heart of the stony hill, and inside the chamber was a yellow circle, like some sort of miniature sun. From the center chamber, a second tunnel led to the other side of the mountain, exiting out the back.

Earl said in a stunned whisper, "This can't be real."

Tim looked over at him and held out the arrowhead. "I don't know about that. Do you see this groove down the center of the arrowhead? That's called a flute. Now, I'm no expert, but I've read

123

enough to know that that's a Clovis Point arrowhead, and I think it might be genuine."

Jay looked at him confused. "You're sayin' that like it's supposed to mean somp'in to me."

Puffing out his chest and speaking in his best professor voice, Tim began to rattle off facts. "The Clovis people are named after the city of Clovis New Mexico where they found the first points in 1929. The points have been found across North America and in all kinds of shapes, but they all share the same distinctive fluting style."

Again, Jay just gave him a flat look. "So these are, what? Native people we're talking about?"

Tim returned the bored look. "That, kid, is an understatement. These aren't just *some* native people. From what all the big wigs can tell, up here in North America the Clovis people are *the* native people. We're talking before the Native Americans, native. We're talking about prehistoric old. *Ice age* old."

That caught his attention. "You're tryin' to tell me that there were some people before the Indians? And they lived all over the U.S, and hunted woolly mammoths and saber tooth tigers? And these people from way back then were painting the same tracks we have in our camp? Christ, how many fuckin' years back is the ice age?"

With a grim expression Tim looked him dead in the eyes and said, "The last ice age, the Younger Dryas, ended about twelve thousand years back. And that's just when it ended. It was around for a lot longer; and it didn't end pretty. Basically a few giant meteors hit an ice sheet that was two miles thick and made a big old ice dam. When the dam broke, it washed out nearly the whole continent. There's a reason there's no more big animals, like mammoths."

"Jesus Christ," breathed Jay, "what the fuck. What in God's name, the actual *fuck* is happening here?"

He took a deep breath to try and steady himself, but as he drew breath, he was met with that strange smell. It was pungent, sour, yet strangely familiar. Jay sniffed the air, trying to place what it was he was smelling. He followed the aroma to a pile of dirt mounded up against the wall. The mound was long, about seven feet or so. It was wide, and the dirt was packed tight. It was coming from here. It was subtle, but it was definitely coming from the dirt mound. Suddenly, the memories from his youth hit him like a truck, and he knew its source. Growing up, he had smelled it far too often from his refrigerator. Hell, even as an adult, the smell of polka dotted meat still haunted his nostrils.

He dug out several scoops of earth at one end, and as soon as the earth was churned, his heart sank. A blend of fear, panic, and sadness fought for dominance as he stared into the sunken, pale face of Mclean. In a voice that he tried to keep steady, he called out, "Mat."

As the group came over, Jay stood up and tried to block the view from Pharrell, but it was too late.

His face changed from curious, to horrified, to pain in a matter of moments. He shoved Jay aside and fell to his knees at the burial mound. His hands trembled as he held them meaninglessly, futilely in front of himself, his face contorted with grief as he tried to comprehend what was in front of him. Suddenly he began frantically burrowing into the compact dirt with his bare hands, pulling back armfuls of it trying to uncover the body. With a shriek, he pulled back, falling onto his side where he curled up in despair.

In the dim light Jay could see that a sheath of flesh and skin had come off the ribs, exposing an open chest cavity underneath. The smell of putrefying muscle and rot erupted from the mound, accompanied by the pungent odor of raw meat. Much of the body seemed to be missing from the grave. His arms and one leg were completely gone; removed and presumably eaten. Jay was no doctor, but he was pretty sure everyone had a heart, even Mclean; at least, he used to. The liver and lungs looked like they were missing too.

All anyone could think to do was cover their mouths and nose with their shirts. Pharrell was still inconsolable on the dirt floor, his wails echoed hauntingly through the cave. No one was sure if it was the stench or the misery of a good man, but all their eyes began to well with tears.

Eventually the grieving moans died down and Mat knelt next to him. He spoke in a slow, soothing voice as he said, "Hey, man, we need to get out of here. I don't know how much longer the torch has."

There was a sniff from the fetal heap. Pharrell shook his head and asked, "Why? Why would they do that to him? Then just bury him here."

Earl was about to speak, but Mat shot him a look that shut him down immediately. "I don't know, man. This world is full of... sometimes the world just takes shit from you. Sometimes it doesn't make sense, but right now we have a torch that's about to go out and we need to get back to camp. We need to leave here."

Pharrell lurched up, his red eyes wide. "We aren't leaving him! Not here. Not like this."

Mat's voice grew stern, but still trying to keep the comforting tone. "Pharrell, I promise you that we will have people come back for him, but right now we have to go get help."

Now he faced those sad, puppy eyes, the kind that tore down the sternest defenses and could melt even the iciest of hearts. That innocent face that pleaded without ever saying a word, but now was no time for innocent hopes.

"What are you going to do, Pharrell? Carry him in your pockets?"

He quickly stole a glance at the bed sheets. He was about to suggest something, but Mat cut him off.

"You think dragging him home with piss-stained bed sheets in the hot sun for miles, and over mountains and rocks is any better?"

Poor Pharrell looked to each of them in turn, each one saying more with their eyes than words ever could. He looked desperately around the cave, then at the torch, then finally to the remains. He visibly sunk and looked like he might lose himself again, but instead he stood. Without looking at any of them, he simply walked purposefully back through the cave; his resolve, broken.

They filed out after him, none of them wanting to spend another second in that long-forgotten pit.

Jay was the last to leave. As he passed the mouth of the chamber, he could have sworn he heard something. It was faint, but it had sounded like rock scraping against rock. Pausing for just a moment, he turned and looked back. The flashlight was up front and the torch was too far to see back. All his vision could grant him was blackness. Blackness that slowly enveloped him as the group made their exit.

* * * * * * * * *

It moved the boulder, just a little. Just enough to peak. It saw them. They had Fire light this time. It had been a long time since Fire was brought into its nest. It hated them for it. It hated the powerful dark one the most; their Alpha, for he carried the Pain Thunder. He was competition; dangerous.

The Blooded One turned to look back. The Fire was gone, and It knew It was unseen. It didn't bother hiding from The Blooded's gaze. No. No more hiding. It knew how to hunt Tall Ones. It would hunt Tall Ones. They would never bring Fire light into its den ever again.

The Blooded One stood there, looking into the dark with its feeble eyes. Then one of its pack called out to it, "Jeay, yeoo coumeeng?"

The Blooded turned and followed its pack, and It would follow the Blooded. The time of stalking had ended. Now, the hunt had begun in earnest.

Thirteen: Night Terrors

The weather had turned for the worse during their time underground. Now a black and grey cloud stretched across the horizon, and it was on the move directly toward their camp. It was an imposing beast, a veritable mountain range unto itself. It stretched far across the land and rose up far into the heavens. Small raindrops began to sprinkle down as they ran through the forest. The rain was harmless, unimposing, but everyone could feel that things were going to get much worse very soon. Once they returned to camp, they found their resident Cuban, Diego, running all over while warning anyone who would listen to batten down the hatches. He'd witnessed the power of wild storms firsthand, and his warnings were heeded.

After everything was secured and properly stored, Mat called everyone for an announcement. All the men gathered at the center of camp to hear the news. Mat stood up on the harvester and motioned for everyone to settle down. His voice was loud, booming and projected out over the crowd. "Everybody, listen up!" Pockets of the crowd still talked amongst themselves until he bellowed even louder, "I said listen the *fuck* up! It is with great sadness that I have to inform you that today another one of our men was attacked. Upon following the aggressor, we found the remains of Charles Mclean."

Murmurs ran through the crowd like a dull roar.

"Due to concerns for the safety of our workers, that's you, we are closing down this site and we will be getting the authorities to investigate-"

His voice was drowned out with the many angry and scared voices rising up from the crowd.

He raised his hands and after several moments was able to quiet them down. "I understand your concern, don't worry, we will get the authorities to investigate what the hell has been happening around here. Now I'm sure you're concerned how this will affect your work and income. I want to assure you, I am well aware of what this job means for you. We have other sites we're zoned for, and we'll be moving to them as soon as we can. In the meantime, this site is done, but due to the extreme nature of the circumstances you will continue to draw a paycheck in full. This money will come from the company reserves. For today, though, we're cutting out early. Tomorrow we'll gather up all the tools and equipment and then once camp is loaded, we'll shove off. Are there any questions?"

The crowd echoed another murmur or two, but in large it remained silent.

"Alright. Let's get some rest. We've got a lot to do tomorrow."

_ _ _ _ _ _ _ _ _ _

The atmosphere of the camp was strange. Somehow simultaneously energetic and lethargic. Some of the men were spinning wild theories about how there were mountain cannibals with banjos and bad teeth. Others were convinced Sasquatch was lurking in the trees, waiting to snag them in the night. Still others thought aliens were harvesting people for their mad experiments. Jay even overheard one guy talking about how he'd seen a magician mind control people on stage before, and how he thought there was a wizard in the forest abducting people. A few of the others speculated that it was a vengeful spirit that was coming to drag them all to hell.

They were all worried and the fear in the air was palpable, but not for all the same reasons. These people needed this job. Some sent money to families who lived on a shoestring budget. A missed day of work could mean the difference between making ends meet or not. Others concerned themselves with the very real concern that there was a killer out there. Each man worked a dangerous job, but if attention was paid and they followed the rules they could probably get through alive. This, though. This was something else. This was something coming after them, *trying* to kill them. Until now they could just write it off as Mclean getting lost after throwing a fit, but this. This was on a whole other level.

Jay mechanically ate his food. He stole a look around, but didn't see Pharrell. He probably didn't want to be around people right now. Especially ones who would badger him about what happened today, much like Zack was doing now.

"Yo, you saw for-real cave paintings in there? Shit, those things would be older than, like, Rome? That's so fucking sick! And you think these Clover homies painted it?"

Without looking up Tim growled, "Clovis."

"Clovis homies, whatever. And they painted the tracks too? Man, think about it, we'll be the first people to discover a new legendary creature. We'll call it, Bighand!"

Tim cuffed him upside the back of the head. "Skinny, a man's dead. No one here liked that son of a bitch, but he didn't deserve that. Getting taken away. Eaten. Only pedophiles and politicians deserve something like that."

Jay looked up with a sad expression. "There was at least one person who liked him."

"Fucking hell!" Tim growled, throwing his spoon into his bowl, "you all are, fuck... I'm going to bed." He stomped off and slammed his bowl on the counter at the food bus before he tramped off.

Zack made sure he was out of ear shot before he leaned and continued where he'd left off. "Ok, but for real, there's been this sun thing with hands for thousands of years and we've never heard about it until now?"

Earl, who had been quiet until this point, spoke up. "He's right, you know. A man *is* dead, even if we didn't like him. I think we should respect-"

"No, I want to talk about this! A man *IS* dead. We **got** to talk about this. What killed him? Why? What is it going to do next? We need to fucking have an idea of who's gunnin' for us so we can keep another homie from biting it. My K.D is a perfect zero/zero and I'd like to keep it that way."

Jay gave him a confused look. "What's Kaidy?"

Zack simply waved him off. "Kill/death ratio. It's a gamer thing. Look, bad joke, but fo'real? I-do-not-want-to-*fucking*-die."

Earl begrudgingly nodded his understanding. "Ok. We'll talk about it. I've been thinking about it, myself. If this thing really has been around since ice age times, I figure that means one of three things. One, there's a population large enough for them to survive. Two, they have been secluded underground or hibernating for years and years. Three, there's just one really old one and it's never met anyone who lived to tell about it."

A look of concentration spread over Zack's face. After a moment of thinking he spoke up. "Well, I feel like a small population could maybe survive way out here in no man's land. Like Bigfoot does-."

Earl rolled his eyes, but didn't interrupt.

"-but I don't think it's one of those. I mean their named for their feet, not their hands. I guess maybe if it did like bears do and get real fat, it could be on the down low for a few years, but I don't think just one could survive for that long. All the predators and hunters and diseases and natural disasters. Unless this thing is, like, an engineered super being, I figure *something* would have killed it by now."

"Well," Jay said, "whatever it is might not operate like normal. This thing's smarter'n we realize. It preserved its food by burying it somewhere cool an' dry. It had tools. It had a natural bandage."

With a turn of his head Zack asked incredulously, "What?"

"Yeah, when I was a kid there was this civil war exhibit that came to our school. We learn't that they used sugar as somethin' real simple to clean wounds. In the cave there was a bowl with honey an' sap. Honey's just sugar and the sap keeps the wound closed. An' there were tools like bowls an' knives."

"Ok," Zack said, putting his hands up, "maybe it just took the knives and bowls and shit from those old hunters."

Earl shook his head. "But that wouldn't explain the sap bandage. I saw a lot of little stone chips, I think it made the knives in that cave."

"And the arrow heads?"

"Well, a couple of them were broken, so maybe it did get the arrows from hunters. Hell, maybe those were the ones it got shot with back in the day."

Jay had a thought come to him and cut in. "Yeah, you know, as damn near impossible as it might be, this thing's usin' all that Stone Age knowledge, even though steel's been around here for hundreds of years. I'm thinkin' that maybe it's a real old, real tough son of a bitch. 'Cause monkeys can learn just from watching, so if this thing's just been out here in bum fuck nowhere an' hasn't seen a modern human for a few hundred years, it'd likely still be chippin' rocks into knives. And maybe it learnt to avoid humans, 'cause we'd hunt it back in the day; just now it can't avoid us."

Earl put his hands up and shook his head to end the line of thought. "Ok, ok, ok. Until we know more, let's just say it can use tools and there's at least one of them. My second thought is, it only goes after people one at a time. It attacked Mclean when he was alone. It got Alejandro when his buddy wasn't looking, and it went after Pharrell's bus when he was supposed to be the only one in there."

With a shrug Zack said very matter-of-factly, "So we just stay in groups and we should be good."

Jay scoffed. "Tell that to Alejandro."

"Fair."

Earl folded his arms and stared at the table. "One thing I can't figure out though is why they painted it like a yellow circle. These aren't abstract artists, they painted what they saw. They paid attention to the details because the details kept them alive."

Then Jay furrowed his brow as he remembered something. "When Ali was gettin' taken, before the pain hit me like a freight train, I remember seein' a light out there. It was really dim, but when I looked at it I felt damn good. And I mean *real* good. Maybe it's got one of those dangly head lamps, like on them deep sea fish. An' for whatever reason it makes you go all, deer in the headlights, like."

With a slow nod Earl agreed. "Some kind of lure? So, my third thought about all this is it's definitely alive; not some ghost or something. This thing leaves tracks, even if they're freaking weird. It also bleeds, it eats, and we know for sure it pisses. The smell of those bed sheets is going to haunt me."

Zack got a wry smile. "So if it's alive, we can kill it."

"Bingo. Like you said though, if there's just the one, it's going to be a *tough* son of a bitch."

— — — — — — — — — —

After the conversation died down the slow raindrops that had started earlier began to pick up. The rain fell more heavily and could be heard slapping the metal roofs with a steady rhythm. They decided to bed down as the last of the sunlight began to fade and darkness fell.

Entering the bus, they did their best to try to keep quiet, but Tim's hearing was better than they had expected. At the sound of the doors opening he shot up in his bed, wielding a heavy flashlight. Its beam was so bright that it was like looking into the sun itself, which blinded each of them completely. In his signature gravel tone he grumbled, "Agh, it's just you. Lock the bar. I'm going back to sleep."

Everyone was too exhausted from the ordeal that day to stay up any longer. After locking the bar they each flopped down on their respective beds and curled up. They had gotten to their trailer just in time. The storm began to hit with full force and unload a torrent of water from above. The mighty wind howled and tore at the busses, rocking them from side to side. Thunder rolled over the mountains and hail pelted the roof. Jay glanced outside and was amazed to see that the rain was coming down sideways. The wind pummeled the bus, shoving it this way and that, making the rain look like waves rippling in the storm. The whole ordeal reminded him of all the hurricanes he'd ever seen on the news. Diego sure knew his storms.

Despite the tropical-strength storm outside, Jay could clearly hear the sound of loud snoring coming from the mound of blankets that was Earl. Unable to get to sleep himself, he rolled onto his back and stared up at the ceiling. Somehow, the rain began to come down even harder. It was rapid firing on the metal and making an awful clatter. He was tempted to get his ear muffs, but that meant going outside to get to the storage under the bus, and there was no way in hell that was going to happen.

It reminded him of a time when he was young. He didn't remember how old he was, but he was young. His dad was in a rage. He subconsciously touched the scar on the back of his head, feeling the smooth line where his hair never grew back. He remembered running outside bleeding and crying. The rain was warm; hot, even. He remembered hearing the breaking of things and shouting that shook the house, even more than the hot thunder. He had run and hid in the shed; the shed with the tin roof. He remembered hiding under the work table, pulling boxes and paint cans around him to hide. Alone in the dark, he cried, with only a weeping head wound for company. The rain against the roof was nearly deafening. It felt like the world was dropping onto him and only that little shed with the thin tin roof would bring him shelter.

His mind flowed back to his bed. He was breathing heavier as the rain kept falling harder. Tears trickled down his face and into his ears. He didn't care. What was he doing here? Or anywhere? Did he ever have a chance? He spent almost his entire adult life in a cage. K.D. 1/0. He had killed a man, and he had seen another dead man today. Had he killed him too? And he was happy. He was *glad* Mclean was dead. He was *glad* his own father was dead, wasn't he? Was that ok? Was he broken? He had no money, no schooling. He was a million miles from home, and his home was just a reminder that he was broken. A freak. A failure. A murderer.

There was another person out here, somewhere; out there. A killer. Maybe it would be best if they just took him in the night. Walked him into the woods and never walked out. All they would find were his clothes and he'd get buried in some long forgotten cave to rot until the end of time.

In silence. In darkness. In a bus in the woods. In a storm, a man with scars on his body and on his soul quietly sobbed until sleep overtook him.

Though he slept, he was continuously awoken through the night, roused by the pounding rain on an old metal roof. Awakened by thunder that shook the trunk of the cabin as it roared down from the heavens. Awakened by flashes of light as bright as the sun that cracked the sky itself. When he slept, his dreams were no escape. Dark shadows and formless beings haunted him. He would run, but it felt as if he was running through chest high water. A pressure on his chest kept him from taking in vital breath, and when he could, it was thick and cold. He wished to lash out and strike back at the shadows that swarmed around him, but his arms had no strength and each strike was held back by unseen forces, rendering them impotent.

Then the formless dream began to take shape. He was lying in a bed on the charter bus, the same one he'd taken to come to the northwest. He was alone, but the bus was driving through the forest at an impossibly fast speed. The world was still dark and the rain still fell. As he laid there he felt unnaturally still. He wanted to raise an arm, or even twitch a finger, but his body wouldn't respond. He wanted to call out, to scream, to cry, but his body refused to obey. It felt as if an invisible hand had reached down his throat and blocked it with a fist.

His gaze was fixed upward, staring out the window. The moon was waxing, building up to a full moon. Its powerful light was barely able to pierce the curtain of angry clouds, but some of its diminished light shone through. The light silhouetted something at the window. It was just a dark form, but once he'd seen it, his mind began to rapid fire through possibilities, trying to find form for the shapeless mass.

Finally, he sculpted the dark clay into the familiar. It was a gorilla, its face was dark and wide with piercing yellow eyes that housed a simple, but calculating mind. There was something atop its head. Was it antlers? As he tried to puzzle out the shape, it morphed into the deer from his dream from so long ago. Moonlight shone off its pearly white teeth, teeth that were fashioned for cutting meat. Still, the yellow eyes stared into him, boring through him with the intensity of their gaze. Then the shape changed again as the antlers fell slack and became braids. The shape became larger, and with big ears. The pail, lifeless face of Mclean hung in the window, eyes glazed over and milky. The meat on half his face fell away to reveal the white bone beneath. Or was it someone else who looked down on him, now? Once again it morphed and changed. It twisted into the soft, pale, doughy face of the man he'd shot in that bank. Blood was splashed across his marshmallow cheeks and his mouth gaped like a fish out of water as the last of his life drained from his body.

Without warning, a clash of thunder boomed overhead, shaking Jay to his bones. In that same moment the world was turned to day, and a jagged lightning bolt illuminated a new face, but only for the smallest measurement of time; just for a frightening heartbeat. It was a native man. He was full blooded, by the looks of him. The kind of pureblood from before any white settlers landed on these shores. His pronounced cheekbones cast exaggerated and haunting shadows over his face. His masculine, aquiline nose almost touched the glass. His face was stern and his eyes spoke of hatred. His hands were cupped up to his head so that he could look through the window without glare; so that he could look directly at Jay. His thin lipped mouth was turned down in a frown of disdain and contempt. The feature that stood out the most, however, was his age. The man looked like he couldn't be older than his mid-twenties, but all over his face were the marks of healed wounds and deep scars; some of which were like deep canyons that eroded his brow, cheeks and lips.

Then, as the flash faded and darkness returned, and the malefic visage that had hung in his window disappeared into the

137

stormy umbral gloom. For the rest of the night, Jay's slumber was as dreamless as the void.

_____

The morning was cold and Jay's skull felt like someone had clubbed him upside the head. He groaned from the splitting headache as the commotion of the others woke him. He was exhausted, but managed to mumble out, "Wha time's'it?"

Zack had clearly slept well. Uncharacteristically, he was already dressed and practically bouncing around the bus. He leaned over and slapped a drum roll against the window above Jay's head. Then in his best announcer voice, broadcast, "What time is it, Johnny? It's the wakey, wakey hour. Brought to you by *Getting the Hell out of Dodge. Getting the hell out of Dodge,* for when normal retreat just isn't enough."

Still half asleep himself, Tim slapped Zack's leg with the back of his hand and grumbled, "Skinny, knock that shit off. You'll break a window."

A window. The window! Jay's dream from the night before came flooding back to him. "Ugh," he groaned as he sat up, shielding his eyes from the diffuse light of day, "I had the weirdest dream. I was gettin' chased by monsters, then there was some creepy Indian guy lookin' through our window at me. It was, somethin' else, I tell you."

Tim rubbed the sleep out of his eyes and asked, "Dot, or feather?"

"Feather. Yeah, he was lookin' right through... there..." he said pointing at the window. Where his finger indicated, the window was smudged with grease and dirt. Jay froze, his blood draining from his face and going cold. "No fuckin' way."

He jumped out of bed, jammed his feet into his boots and half staggered, half ran outside. The window to the bus was close to eight feet off the ground, but plain as day, underneath the smudged

138

window was a set of human hand prints. The palms were sunk deep into the mud under the window. It had come to him in the night. It had been here.

The ground was still soaking wet from the heavy storm the night before, and the roof of clouds overhead had lowered overnight. The world, it seemed, had been swallowed by a fog so dense it almost felt as if he were breathing underwater.

From the window, the trail of prints disappeared into the fog, heading deeper into the camp. Tentatively he stalked after the trail, compelled and mesmerized by curiosity.

Zack poked his head out of the bus and asked, "What's happening, Jay man?"

Jay waved him down and mimed a shushing motion.

Seeing the trail, Zack's eyes went wide. He scrambled to get his boots on and followed after Jay. "Bro, are those them?"

Jay angrily mimed again for him to keep quiet. He nodded toward the path, and the pair stalked into the hazy miasma. Step by step, the smog revealed the muddy trail until the shadowy outline of Mat's trailer came into view. At the sight of it, Jay's heart dropped and his blood ran cold. It felt like a block of lead rested on his chest and his skin prickled painfully.

The flimsy door to the trailer was desperately holding on by a single hinge. The metal joint creaked with a long, piercing wail as it wobbled lifelessly in its frame. The antenna for the SAT phone had been savagely ripped from the roof and now lay in several pieces, scattered throughout the mud and mangled beyond repair. They got closer, stepping as silently as they could. Giving a look back at Zack, they shared an understanding nod and crept inside.

Evidence of the intruder was clear, as there were muddy handprints all over the course carpet. The inside had been trashed, just like the bus previously. Cupboards were open or torn off their hinges. Papers were littered on the table and floor, carelessly thrown about. The bed sheets were missing and in the back, several items of clothes had been tossed as carelessly as the papers had. In the whole trailer there was no sign of Mat.

It had taken him. It had to have, what else could this be? They had to get him back, but how? Then a thought hit Jay like lightning. The gun! He rushed over to the safe. On the ground in front of it was a large rock and one of their axes. The safe had several dents and deep scratches where the black paint had been chipped off, but it had held up to the brutalization from the simple tools. With the dial in his hand he was about to enter the combination, when he realized something paramount. He didn't know the safe number, and if it was written down anywhere they were never going to find it in time.

Just as he began to surrender to despair, another thought came. This one came more like a slow trickle of molasses rather than a bolt of energy. It started as a little tugging on the back of his mind until it had globbed up to become something substantial. He focused on it and allowed it to come in its own time.

It was something Mat had said, but not recently. It was when he first got here. No, it wasn't *what* he said, it was *how* he said it. It was about the safe; its combination. Mat had paused when he said it was locked. No, he had paused when he said only *he* knew the combination. Why did he pause? Because he had a thought, that's why. Only *he* knew the combination; but was that true? He had grown up with Mat. They knew everything about each other back then. Phone numbers? Too long. Graduation? Not important enough, and they were at different schools by then. Bank information? That wouldn't cause a pause. Birthdays? Only, it would be easy for someone to do some digging and find out Mats' birthday. But what if...?

Jay smiled to himself and started turning the dial.

Zack peeked over his shoulder with a look of amazement as he heard a click, followed by the heavy iron door swinging open. "I call hacks," he breathed.

Jay stood up, retrieved the rifle and began his weapons check. "No, just good reasonin' and a little bit of insight. Well, maybe a lottle-bit of insight, and luck."

"You got a plan?"

"Yup. Get the gun, kill the fucker dead, get my buddy back, and live happily ever after."

"Ok, I'm with you on the goal, but trust, I've seen raids go down in flaming shit because people didn't have a plan. We don't need a Leroy, we need strats."

Jay gave him a confused look. "Son, sometimes I think you're talkin' a whole other language."

Shouting came from outside and they rushed to see the commotion, rifle in hand. It was easy to find out what caused the shouting. The heavy rain from the night before had caused a mudslide. The compacted dirt road was gone, replaced by enough trees to build a dozen homes, enough mud to fill the homes, and a couple of car sized boulders mixed in for good measure.

Jay looked up the embankment, now stripped of features. There was, of course, a bald strip on the land where a thick strip of it had been torn away, but that wasn't what drew Jay's attention. It was the trees along the side of the bald strip. The trees had all fallen downhill, all pointing toward one spot. They had fallen in such a way so as to act like a funnel, channeling the deluge of water into one spot that caused the earth to cascade and slip. All those trees, all the ones that channeled the water, had a very distinctive cut at their base. The funneling trees had been chopped down. This was no act of nature.

"Skinny, you were sayin' you had a plan?"

"Gettin' one. First we need to get the gang."

– – – – – – – – –

It didn't take long for news of Mat's disappearance to spread over the camp, but between the efforts to clear the road and to pack up all the equipment, no one could spare the time to worry. Things had shifted to crisis mode, and the longer they stayed, the more that could go wrong. It was a potentially deadly hike to the closest town, so all effort was directed to clearing the road. Then to compound the issue, everyone's concerns were also plagued by the human devouring entity that stole people in the night. The thoughts consumed everyone, everyone except four men who sat in their bus hatching a plan.

Zack cleared his throat and paced around the living room with his arms resting behind his back. He spoke clearly and confidently, the only thing he was missing was the old pipe and he'd be a regular Sherlock Holmes. "Likely the creature has pinched our homie, Mat, to its evil crib. Now, you told me that you chased it to its place, and inside you peeped that it had had first aid and shit, but the creature, itself, had already split. There is one problem with your conjecture! That room was a dead end. How did the creature pass you? But, what if that final room wasn't, in fact, the final room? Now check this out, yo, what if there was a secret passage behind the bookshelf?"

Jay thought for a moment. "Now that you mention it, I thought I heard somethin' movin' as we were leavin'."

Zack shifted back to his normal, energetic self as he shouted, "Boom! The killer used the secret chamber to give you all the slip and escape, and now it struck again."

Tim grunted. "Get to the point, Skinny."

Zack rolled his eyes and took a seat. "Ok, ok. So, from what you guy's told me about the paintings and everything, I think there's a passage that goes all the way through. The chamber you guy's found is in about the middle of the mountain and that pool is where the lava would have pushed up and out, but then it filled in with water. The cave is tight, so if we go all SWAT style, we'll lose the numbers advantage. Plus if we start trying to cap this thing we might bring the whole cave down on top of us. So, I figure we lure it out, then one of us slips in and the rest of us block the cave so it can't follow. That leaves three of us in the woods with the gun and one person alone inside to get Mat. If he's hurt you can use the blankets in there to drag him. Then the cave team can bail out on the other side of the mountain. We'll meet up and head back to camp. This thing doesn't deal with groups, we just need to stay in groups."

142

Earl sat with his hands clasped, nervously. "Just one big problem, how do we lure it out?"

Zack suddenly became very interested in cleaning the dirt from his fingernails. In a quieter voice he mumbled, "I think someone is going to have to go in, alone..."

The table was silent. Everyone just looked at him.

"I mean, think about it. It's a predator, and predators chase things. A cat can't *not* chase a mouse. It's a compulsion."

They all wanted to argue the point, but none of them could. Were there better plans? Probably. Were there safer plans? Definitely, but time was against them. Jay nodded to himself and slammed his hand onto the table. "Earl, do you think you can find the cave again?"

Earl nodded. "Yeah, no problem."

Jay turned to Tim next. "Can you still handle a rifle?"

The grizzled man gave a throaty, "Ha! I was in the 100 meter Dime Club back in the day. Probably couldn't do it now, but I remember which end the bullets come out of."

Finally he turned to Zack who held his hands up before Jay could even speak. "You don't even need to ask. I'm in. I'll pull the boss; I mean, lure out the monster."

With a shake of his head Jay spoke in a somber tone. "No, you've got a future, but we'll need as many hands as we can get for the team outside. Besides, this thing... it does somethin' to you. To your head. I know what it feels like so I think I can bull through it if I'm expecting it. I'll lure it out, then you three keep tight."

No one liked it, but options were thin. They all agreed and prepared. Earl made a bundle of torches, Tim ran the rifle through its paces, Zack loaded a backpack full of supplies, and Jay pocketed his tiger handle knife, Tim's club of a flashlight, and picked through the tools in the work shed. If this thing wanted a fight, it found one.

Fourteen: Follow The Leader

Gathered in silence, the group hiked to the cave without a single word. Even the forest seemed to be mute. The quietness only added to the unnerving and seemingly unnatural presence of the fog that surrounded them. It had become so thick that they had to practically swim through it. For all they knew the tops of trees didn't even exist and they just reached up forever into the sky like the five pillars at the end of all things. Or maybe the world ended a hundred feet in any direction and they would find the edge if they just kept walking. Or perhaps they were already dead and this endless sea of mist was purgatory. No matter, spirits were low enough already without the extra weight of thoughts like that. They all felt the fear that would make most men turn tail, but each of them, to a man, was determined.

They arrived at the cave, its solitary tree looming like a watchtower. The hike up had been brisk and they were all winded. They huddled behind a boulder to catch their breath. Earl gave Jay a torch from the bundle he carried.

Jay took the torch in one hand and Tim's hefty club light in the other. "Ok, Y'all know where you'll hold up?"

Earl nodded. "Once you're in, we'll mount the boulder, the big one up the hill, and hold there. It's close enough that we can cover the cave, and it's open enough that we can defend it. I figure we surround it with a few torches and we'll be alright on the high ground. Tim will have line of sight and if it gets close..." he held up his double sided ax.

"Good. Zack?"

With an all too happy grin, he held up a spear made from sharpened rebar.

With a nervous roll of his neck, Jay set his jaw and said, "Alright, if I don' come shootin' out of there in thirty minutes, get the hell back to camp and get out of here. We don' need to lose people if we don' need to."

With that, they all crept up the hill, over rocks, and into position. Jay looked up one last time as Earl got up to the tree above the mouth of the tunnel. Earl met his gaze and said, "I'll pray for you."

Jay lit the torch with a lighter and turned on the flashlight. Armed with a head full of fool's courage and little else, he ducked and entered into the dark.

In this place, his mind swirled. He tried to remember each rock and pillar as they came, but confused them once they were out of sight. He needed to know the cave if he was going to run through it; literally for his life. He was glad for the torch. It was warm, and the deeper he traveled the colder he became. He had been sweating hard on the hike over, and the cold air tore the heat from his body with unforgiving fingers. His muscles burned from the exertion, but his time of living like a mountain man had made him stronger; strong enough to keep pushing on.

Jay approached the narrowest section of the cave. The passage was almost completely blocked where stalagmite and stalactite kissed, growing into a single barrier of stone. To pass between the narrow section between the pillar and the wall. Jay exhaled all his breath to push beyond.

Once he was on the other side, he shone the powerful flashlight around, sweeping it over rock walls and cold floors, making sure there was no lurking horror.

Satisfied that he was alone, he pushed on, descending into the depths until he came to a familiar bend. He knew the next passage would lead to the lair. Jay took a long breath to steady his nerves. Then, when he was ready, he whipped the light up and blasted it down the hall, ready to blind anything that might lay in ambush.

To his relief, the cave ahead was empty. Slowly, he crept toward the chamber until he was at its proverbial door. He thrust the flaming stick in front of him and slashed through the air, trailing wild arcs of fire and flinging droplets of molten sap. Again, though, the room was empty. Stalking into the cavity he found clean bed sheets layered on top of the old soiled ones, with several items of clothing littered around an uneaten pair of boots. It had been here, but where was it now? And where was Mat? There was no fresh meat being left out to dry, so that was a good sign.

He was sure it was here though, somewhere. It was far too easy for his mind's eye to see it in every flicker of shadow the torch cast. Every sense Jay possessed was working overtime. His ears were sharpened to the slightest sound. The breath that escaped his lips and the heart in his chest was a cacophony inside the silent stillness. The air was putrid with rot, even though the body had been covered and packed once again. The smell was slightly better near the pool of water in the grotto, but not enough to dampen the horrendous smell.

Jay lay the torch in the center of the room to fully illuminate it and to free up a hand. While he explored, he had decided that he wouldn't let his eyes adjust to the darkness. What good would it do? Down here there was light, or there was not. The creature would have to adjust if he surprised it, and that moment of adjustment might mean the difference between life and death.

After some brief investigation, he found what he was looking for. An inconspicuous rock on the far side of the chamber near the large mural. The boulder was pretty substantial in size, and Jay didn't think he could move it by himself, but the stone lay ajar and revealed another tunnel leading out of the room.

The hole was little more than a small portal, almost perfectly round and slightly more than half his height. He crouched down, his thick jeans making far too much noise for his liking as they crumpled and folded around his legs. He was about to shine the light in, when he heard it. He heard, *It*, and the sound of flesh slapping stone. It was a small noise, but it hit him like a truck and made his heart skip a beat. He pushed the head of the flashlight into his chest to kill the light, so that he didn't have to click its deafening off button.

As silently as he could, he scrambled around the rock. He was sure the mad pounding of his heart against his ribs would give him away, but there was nothing he could do. He tried to slow his breath, taking as slow, and controlled breaths as a man panicked to the edge of madness could. Still worried the light would give him away, he dug the head of the flashlight harder against his chest, making sure *no* light would escape.

At first, he wasn't sure if he'd just been hearing things, but then validation came in the form of a frightening and unholy sound that echoed from the darkness. He wasn't going to take any chances, and remained frozen. It couldn't have been more than a second or three, but it felt like a hundred years of listening before he heard it again. It was a slow, evenly paced rhythm, like the measured gait of a suspicious denizen coming home to find something out of place; and it was getting closer. The gentle, soft, unmistakable slap, slap, slapping of hands against stone. Each step was cautious and methodical. Each slap grew louder and louder until he could tell that the source of the sound was right at the mouth of the chamber. Then it stopped. It stopped for so long, Jay was sure he was caught. Of course, it knew he was there, his torch was just lying there, washing light over a place that light was never meant to touch.

Then it took a step, and then silence. Once again there was a single step, and then another. He could hear it walk tentatively into the chamber. His muscles ached and burned while small rocks dug into his knee, but he didn't dare move. He gambled by even drawing breath.

Then it came into view. He was still pressed against the rock with all his might, trying to be as small and unseen as possible. All he could see was the head as it revealed itself around the edge of his hiding place. The creature stepped into the center of the room, and it was frightening. Its face was the same as the native man from his dream. The native man with the hard eyes, the stern lips, and deep scars that told of countless battles past. The head, though it was like that of a man's, was larger than any normal human he'd seen, and it was terribly wrong. It stuck out long ways, with its neck out of view, as if the head were supported from behind instead of underneath, lingering off of some still obscured body. The fire under its face lit his fierce features with living orange light. The shadows and the flickering flames that danced across its face bestowed an aura of true evil to the figure. From its head, two long, black braids hung down and swung limply in the air, dangling and swinging as the head turned to observe the chamber.

Its eyes looked high around the room and it failed to notice him as he pressed himself deeper down into the corner. A thick, calloused hand emerged from around the corner as it reached out, but the appendage emerged from far too low to belong to a human. It grasped the torch and Jay was able to see more of the beast. The hand was human, with fingers more than twice as thick as a normal man's, and with weathered skin. Strangely, a tight, short fur began to grow abruptly at the naked wrist, and grew up the forearm and out of view.

The fiend lifted its head up toward the ceiling. As it took in a breath to fill its lungs, its lips peeled back to reveal a mouthful of squat, triangular canines. Then it bellowed. An unearthly wail erupted from its husky throat. It was a sound that no man nor natural beast had uttered since creation. The hell song pierced his ears and felt like an audible rasp that shaved against his mind. Although the shriek was so alien and so unearthly, its message was clear. It was a challenge; a call to battle, like a bugle blast from days of old.

Then it lifted the torch with disdain, and it threw the lonely light into the water, extinguishing it. Darkness consumed them both and the cave became blacker than the blackest of nights.

Then it sniffed.

Jay felt like his blood abandoned him as it emptied from his face. His eyes bulged. His scalp tingled and his body screamed for him to run, but he fought it. All he allowed himself to do was take a silent gasp of air, and nothing more. No more breathing, no sound, nothing.

It sniffed again. Then he heard the soft clap of skin on stone. It sampled the air once more. Sniff. Clap. Clap.

It was getting closer. Then a sound, a soft sound; softer than before. It was stepping so lightly, the noise was almost imperceptible as it tried to mask its movements. His lungs began to tighten as he held his breath, his body reflexively tried to pull in air, but he closed his throat. Not a sound.

In the blackened belly of the mountain, there was no wisp or clatter; not from him, and not from it. The stagnant air hung still, tickling his nostrils. The oppressive silence pressed down, and the claustrophobic darkness strangled him more than his quickly depleting breath.

It sniffed again.

He could feel the air brush against his face as it was sucked up the nostrils of the gluttonous thing. It was a mere inch away from his own face.

He shrieked, far more shrill than he ever intended, and reflexively whipped the light up. The miniature sun blasted the demon in the face to reveal a flash of teeth, eyes, and fur as it shrieked back in pain and surprise. In the split second that it was illuminated, he was able to make out an enraged face upon a terrifyingly large body with spindly, flailing limbs.

He heard it stumble and shriek. More on reflex than thought, Jay wildly lashed out with the end of the flashlight as he leapt, explosively, from his crouching stance. With all the force he could bring to bear, he struck it across the face, bashing the side of its head and stumbling it as he sprinted past toward the far side of the chamber. As he clambered into the passage, he heard the nightmare beast hit the ground hard. It shrieked again and he heard the scrambling of flesh against stone as it righted itself. It gave a throaty hiss and roared. The chase was on.

All thought was gone. He didn't even remember he had a plan. All he knew was that forward was life and all else was death. The sound of snarls and padded hands against stone reminded him every second of what followed in that tunnel. With hunger, fury, and madness the creature surged after him; so it was with fury and madness that Jay ran. He launched himself through the tight spaces, scraping his skin against the rough stone, and although he clawed himself terribly, he felt none of it in his blind panic. He would trip, stumble, and bash himself against the rocks, only to rise up with the speed and haste of a hunted rabbit. The cold air of the cave cracked his lips and throat and he began to taste blood, but he surged on.

150

The creature must have been used to traversing the cave slowly, because in its mad dash it stumbled and tripped in the dark far more than Jay, and it had to wriggle through the choke points with more hardship than he had managed.

Somehow, mercifully, he saw a light far ahead of him. With burning muscles, he charged up the tunnel. His lungs and throat were so raw he could taste the powerful metallic taste of blood, but onward he ran. He dropped his flashlight and with bare hands crawled and scrambled toward the light. Behind him he could hear feral snarling like that of a rabid dog. The sounds chased him and propelled him to push harder. Light was almost within reach.

With a burst of speed and the last of his power, he erupted from the mountain's maw and tumbled down the rocky embankment like a ragdoll. He heard something above him, snarling. Then a gunshot and a large, furry body flew over him as he tumbled to a stop. There was another explosive blast from the rifle, and the sound of rocks and branches crashing down the mountain slowly faded away.

Choking on dust and coughing for air, Jay somehow found the strength to push himself up and began to crawl up to the cave.

After a few moments Earl came stomping down the mountain, careful not to cause a rockslide. With one arm, he helped pick up his friend from the dust. "You came flying out of there like a bat out of hell!" Earl said as he quickly looked him over, "shit, man, you're in a bad way."

Jay looked down at himself and coughed. "I might be a little banged up, but I made it. Maybe prayers *do* work," he joked. His clothes were torn and his skin was scratched and bruised. After dusting himself off, he said, "I'll be fine. Did we get it?"

"No. Tim got off two shots, but it blew out of there too fast. Once the first shot went off, it booked it toward the trees."

Jay was bent over, catching his breath. He hocked a loogie and spat, trying to clear his throat of all the dirt he'd swallowed. "Did you get a good look at it?"

Earl shook his head. "Sorry, it happened so fast; and with this fog? All I saw was a shape and some fur. It was big, though. Real big."

That worried Jay. "What, like, is it people sized?"

"It was more like a bull, man. Maybe I saw it wrong, but trust me, it's not small."

With an exacerbated sigh, Jay still hurt, but he was about rested enough to get moving again. People were still in danger. He paused for a moment and thought; then nodded and said, "Alright, we move ahead with the plan. Keep the high ground, light the torches. I don't think it likes fire. You've got your radio?"

Earl took it from his belt and shook it, showing the affirmative.

"Alright, good. I'll take a torch an' a pack, then head back in. Seal it up behind me so that thing don't slip. We'll radio you when we come out the other side. Good luck."

Earl patted him on the shoulder. "Good luck to you, too, buddy."

And with that Jay lit up another torch. With a steel heart and grit teeth, he stepped back into the mountain's jaws.

There were several loud thuds of metal biting into wood behind him. The impacts shook dirt from the entrance until the solitary tree creaked and crashed down, sealing him in. He easily managed to find the flashlight he'd dropped. Looking it over, he thanked God it still worked. No going back now.

— — — — — — — — — —

Traveling through the cave again was agony. His muscles were fatigued and each step felt like fire. To add to his woes, the pain from his wounds was beginning to register as the adrenaline wore off. Another side effect of the loss of adrenaline was that his hands and legs began to shake uncontrollably, which didn't improve his situation. Because of his new pack, he was heavier now, too. At least now he had supplies. He wanted to rest, to sleep, to eat, and forget about the world; even for a little bit, but that wasn't an option. All he allowed himself was one of the bottled waters and a power bar.

Eventually he made it back through the cave and to the lair. He sat on the rock table to catch his breath. Reluctantly, he didn't let himself rest long, for he knew he'd never get back up again if he got comfortable. All he needed was enough rest to let the tension out of his muscles for a second. He took a breath, filled his lungs to burst, and was reminded of why he chose here to rest. The smell was putrid and he quickly found the motivation to keep going.

The cave on this side of the mountain was essentially the same as the other; dark, rocky, and cold. He kept his ears open, but let his mind wander so that he didn't have to feel his body. He decided to ponder the cave paintings. Under different circumstances he would have loved to have lingered to admire them. He always liked art. He never thought he was good at it, but he liked it. He even took a painting class when he was in prison. The teacher said he had potential, but Jay didn't see it. He'd gotten decent at whittling, over the last few weeks. Maybe he just needed practice. Maybe if he survived this he'd try his hand at painting again. His mind meandered back to the cave wall. He imagined them coming to life, or *back* to life. All those strange and exotic beasts roaming the wild lands. The rich colors of the paints had made them so realistic, and they had ignited his imagination.

Suddenly, jarringly, he was snapped back to reality by the sound of a distant cough. His heart jumped as he was pulled from the colorful grass lands and herds of primeval animals back into the dark cave. Tentatively, he called out, "Mat, Mat is that you?"

His voice echoed through the cave, and for several moments it was only his own voice that echoed back. Then came a weak, "Jay?"

"Yeah, yeah it's me!"

New life found him and he doubled his pace down the old lava tube. In his haste he almost didn't register Mat's voice until it was too late.

"There's a hole. Jay. Look out, *the hole!*"

At the last second Jay stopped. He found himself standing at the lip of a drop off that was nearly invisible in the gloom. He looked down and was met with a grizzly sight. The pit was a dumping ground of bones and debris. Scraps of cloth, skulls of beasts, long bones, teeth, hooves, antlers, pelts and a myriad assortment of skeletons covered in dried blood and dirt. Sweeping the light over it all, Jay couldn't see his friend. "Mat? You down there? You ok?"

Then from under a ledge, the head of his friend poked out. "Me? Oh, I'm peachy," he said sarcastically, "a pile of jagged bones broke my fall. I'd say I'm glad to see you, man, but all I see is that fucking bright-ass light." His voice was shaking and sounded strained. There was a tremble to it that betrayed Mat's bravado.

Jay pointed the flashlight upward at the ceiling, letting its beam scatter and bathe the cave in a gentler light. "What're you doin' down there? Is anythin' broke?"

Mat was laying on his back under the shelf and began to hastily shuffle out from underneath. "Na, man. I was in my trailer last night and there was a bang from outside. Then everything went kind of hazy." Having successfully exited from under the shelf, he sat up and began to scramble out of the pit with haste. The pit seemed much deeper than it really was, only being about eight feet down. It was thin and long, almost like a small chasm. "All I can remember after that is being in this cave. This suffocating, fucking cave. I came to when I fell into this hole. After I fell I heard a bunch of scary fucking animal sounds above me so I hid. I wasn't about to fight something with rabies in the dark," he said as he pulled himself out. He was visibly sweating, which Jay doubted was from exertion. "That hole was *way* too fucking small."

Jay tried to lighten the mood and said, "Ah, quit your cryin' you muscly baby. Now get your ass movin'. Tim, Earl an' Zack are held up at the other end and they're waitin' on us."

"What the hell's going on, man?"

"Come on, I'll explain on the way."

Fifteen: Outer Demons

The explanation was short, and the mission was, so far, successful. Spirits were high and travel was short. The journey through the second cave took less time than the first. Once they reached the back exit, it became clear why the cave with the tree was the front door. Moonlight spilled through a hole in the ceiling at the end of the cave. At some point long ago the roof must have collapsed to reveal the outside world. Moss hung down from the lip above and ferns grew along the wall where clumps of dirt clung to the stone.

As the pair began their climb, Jay was silently thankful that he didn't have to drag Mat out. Unless he had a sled and a crane, he doubted he'd be able to get it done. It wasn't a long climb, but it was a slow one. The rocks were wet from the mist above and more than once a drop of condensed water fell off a rock and into their eyes. In time, the pair managed to haul themselves out of the pit and back into the limbo that was the eerie, vaporous, green mountains.

It was after sundown, now. The hike had eaten up most of the day, and his adventures below the earth must have finished off the rest. The miasma-like fog diffused the heavy light from the full moon, making the night glow with a preternatural luminosity.

Mat breathed a sigh of relief and opened his arms to the wide-open world, thankful to be out of his confines. Jay, however, was still on edge. He was nagged by the ever-present possibility that the beast, whatever it was, hadn't stuck to their plan. Perhaps it was less animal than they had presumed. Perhaps it possessed the abstract ability to overcome its compulsory nature and disengage. Perhaps it figured out their plan and it was coming around the mountain to catch them at this end, tired and vulnerable.

Jay pushed the thoughts from his mind. Speculating didn't change things. It either ran away and wasn't their problem, was engaged with the other team, or was coming for them now. He hoped for the best, but prepared for the worst. The safe option was to assume that it had come for them and was already here waiting for its moment. If he thought like that, it couldn't surprise them.

He keyed his radio and called out to the other team, "Jay to Earl, I've got Mat and we're out of the tunnel. Comin' back to you now. Over."

The radio crackled and a jumbled message came back, but it was too scrambled to make sense of. At least there was a reply. This way he knew they were still alive. If the radio was a bust, then it was time to get moving.

He looked around for a moment and found a long stick. He broke the end off at a slant and hastily ground the end into a rough point against a rock. He tossed the makeshift spear to Mat and then made another for himself, all the while keeping his head on a swivel, eyes scanning every leaf and bush.

Alert and armed, they pushed onward and began their journey to circumnavigate the mountain. Jay was in the lead because he knew their destination. Mat could clearly see how rough his friend had had it and was letting Jay set the pace.

Jay's spear doubled as both a walking stick and a paddle while they swam through the sea of shrubs and trees. The bushes were enumerable, tall, and thick. It was an exhaustive labor to push through them and each time they did it seemed like they made enough noise to wake the dead. Paradoxically, the intensely shaking foliage was a strange relief to the beleaguered journeyman. If there was a creature closing in for the kill, they could hear it coming a mile away. Less comforting, however, was the way each branch clawed at his already abused skin.

Every foot they traveled felt like a mile, but with time and caution they were able to make it to the rocky slope of the other side without incident or an encounter with the thing. They had miscalculated slightly and wound up much higher than they needed to be. Through the thick clouds of mist they could see the flickering light of torches burning below them, though the flames were reaching the end of their lives. Several had clearly burned out already, as the only parts left were dimly glowing charcoal.

The descent was treacherous, and the ground slid out from underneath them, but the crumbling earth held enough, and they were able to get to the truck sized boulder that the others were holding out on.

Upon scrambling atop the boulder, it was apparent that the situation was grim. Tim was out cold, laying on the rock with a blood-stained shirt tied tightly around his head.

Earl was sitting shirtless next to him with all his weight on one knee while he gripped the rebar spear. His other leg stuck out and was wrapped with his bloody shirt, with two strong sticks to keep it straight.

Zack was shirtless as well and holding the rifle tightly against his shoulder, aiming around wildly. Deep cuts and richly colored bruises dotted his face, back, and chest. They heard Jay and Mat's approach and whirled around, ready to fight.

Fortunately, Zack had enough sense to look first and shoot second. "*Fucking* about *time*! Jay, it's going bad, man. It's smart, and it's fucking quiet. It crept up and threw a rock at Tim's head, and I mean it was a *rock*. Thing must have been the size of a melon! We can't wake him up."

Earl groaned as he shifted his weight. "Yeah, then Skinny here stabs me in the leg with his Goddamn spear, may He forgive me."

"Dude! You were walking off the rock like a zombie. The fuck else was I gonna do?"

Jay looked at the gashes and purple splotches on Zack's body.

Zack followed his gaze and said, "Oh, these? Yeah, fucker hasn't stopped throwing rocks. Thug and buggin' little bitch."

Jay checked to make sure Tim was still breathing. He was alive, but they couldn't stay here. "When'd ya see it last?"

"Maybe five minutes ago. It got me in the back with a rock the size of my foot. I think it might be getting tired. It was no-

159

scoping when Tim went down, but I've been dodging for a while and it's getting sloppy, but I'm not at a hundred percent either."

Jay grumbled. "At least we're *all* in bad shape. We can't stay here. Mat, you're closer to a hundred than any of us, think you can handle Tim?"

Mat nodded and lifted the unconscious man into a fireman's carry over his broad shoulders.

"Earl, how's the leg? Think you can walk with some help?"

With a groan of effort, he propped himself up and held out a hand. "Let's find out."

It was slow and painful, but they managed to get him to his feet. Though once he was up, the big man proved to be far too much to handle in Jay's drained state. They began to fall, but Mat was able to nudge them back up with his hip.

Jay steeled himself and mustered all the strength he had left. From between clenched teeth, he was able to grunt out, "Zack, help."

The young man slung the rifle and quickly added his support. "I got him, I got him. You take the rifle."

That little bout of lifting had winded Jay and sapped every last ounce of his strength. He sucked down air like a dying man and with heavy, clumsy hands he slid the rifle off Zack's back. Back in his day he'd held a rifle or two, so he was used to their weight and feel. Now, though, it felt as if he was trying to lift an entire tree. Lethargy gripped him and he wanted nothing more than to just drop everything and fall.

But if he did, then the creature would come and eat him. Then it would eat the only people who'd ever shown him real kindness. Forcing his tenth wind, he lifted the weapon. They needed him now and he wasn't going to fail them.

Ready to head out, they climbed down the rock with care. Each step was arduous, but step after step they managed to make it down the rocky embankment to the forest. During the descent Jay had lingered at the back while Mat plowed ahead like a steam

160

engine. Jay thought he might get whiplash with how fast and paranoid he was looking around.

Too absorbed with covering the ground, Jay was slow to register the rustling from above in the trees. Too late, he realized the danger. The stone came down hard against his skull. In the first instant it was like his vision was bounced back into his head. His sight darkened and the world elongated before it rebounded like a rubber band. Then the world darkened into total blackness. A moment later he awoke on the ground. There were people around him shouting his name, but he didn't recognize the voices at first.

He could see them looking down, but he didn't recognize their faces either. He could see their mouths open and their lips move. He could hear the sounds they made, and he could understand his name, but everything else was Jabberwocky.

Then things started to come back into focus as Mat screamed, "Jay, you have to get up! Jay, we can't leave you here!"

He propped himself up. Using the rifle, he was able to stand on shaking legs. His eyes were half lidded and a patch of blood smeared the side of his head. Strangely, he felt awash with a sense of calm. A bizarre clarity had gifted him the perfect sight to see what he needed to do. Speaking more to himself than to anyone, he whispered, "Leave me here."

"What? Jay, are you ok? We need to keep moving. Get your ass in gear, come on!"

The rifle felt light, now. It didn't feel like anything. Nothing felt like anything. He looked at them. These people. That's all they were, people; and he wasn't. He had become abstract. Jay was no longer Jay. Jay didn't exist. He was an opportunity. An opportunity to save lives.

He looked at them with an expressionless face and in a monotone voice he said, "You have to leave. You all have to leave. You have to leave me here."

Mat was looking around like a wild man. "Jay, this is not the time for this. We're vulnerable out here. Let's go!"

Still expressionless he just looked at the large man. "Why? To go home? I am home, but you're not. You have a business. Earl has a family. Tim has a skill. Zack has a future." As the last word passed his lips all of his missing motions flooded back into him. His voice choked and the tears blinded him. He squeezed them out of his eyes until they were like waterfalls down his cheeks. He became frenzied and screamed, "**I have nothing, Mat! I don't have *none* of those things, not'a one!** All I've got are four people in the whole world that can look me in the eye, and they're gonna die if they stay here. I have the gun, I have a chance. I'll be alone. It'll come for me."

Mat hefted Tim's body more squarely on his shoulders and looked Jay dead in the eye. His voice was firm, direct and focused. "Jay. We are *not* leaving you."

"Seriously, homie. Are you fucking stupid?"

"Jay, I think I can speak for Tim, too, when I say there's no way."

Jay was hysterical, and it took every ounce of his focus to stay standing. His body trembled and his breath was sporadic, borderline hyperventilating. His head felt light, and everything was dizzy. "I can't walk; I can barely stand. Y'all can either go slow until you're picked off, or you can carry my ass, and I don't think you've got enough arms."

They each looked at the other in turn, every one of them wore a grim expression. Every one of them wanted to argue, to come up with another option, a reason to drag him along. No plan presented itself, and time wouldn't allow them even a second more. A branch snapped off in the distance and a decision had to be made.

There was a shimmer in Mat's eyes as he turned to his friend. Jay simply gave an up nod, telling them to go. The only response Mat could give, was to set his jaw and nod his understanding.

The group turned into the fog and stomped off between the trees, double time. They weren't about to let his sacrifice be in vain. After several minutes the sounds of their crashing through the

162

brush subsided until the only sounds were silence. There were no birds here, there were no squirrels chasing each other. There were no bugs flying and buzzing past his ears. The air was still, save for long, wispy tendrils of smoky mist that curled around the trunks of trees.

Jay set his back against one of the trees and hung his head. He closed his eyes and cradled the rifle. There was no plan. He was just going to eat up as much of this thing's time as he could; probably while it ate *him*. He'd shoot it if he could, but he knew that wasn't going to happen. If it hadn't been shot yet, what chance did he have? No, he was done. He felt calmer about it than he thought he should. Maybe he was confusing calm with hypoglycemia. Heh, there was another big word that stuck with him. He'd seen more than a few people back home struggle with being a Texan with diabetes, and low blood sugar could get dangerous. The power bar he'd eaten earlier sure as hell wasn't going to cut it after all this. Hell, even if he made it back he'd probably slip into a coma or something.

Then a throaty, haunting voice suddenly broke the silence. "Jeayhee."

His blood turned arctic. The unearthly sounds that caressed his ears stimulated the most primeval parts of his mind. His instincts screamed at him to run. He squeezed his eyes shut. He couldn't run, he couldn't fight, and he couldn't bring himself to look up. To look at it. To look at *It*.

"Jeheee," it called again.

In his desperation, Jay silently pleaded. God, please just make it go away. The thing was calling from a short distance away, and by the sound, there was no mistaking that it was straight ahead. This couldn't be real. He had to have already died. But once it was done with him, then it was going to go for the others. They would die; eaten by this demon. He couldn't let that happen.

He resolved to do this one thing, this one last thing. He had to at least try; at least wound it, something, anything. That strange calmness came to him as his mind stepped outside itself. Time itself seemed to slow. His actions seemed smooth and fluid; even though the whole movement took a fraction of a second. His eyes came up with the rifle. There was no time to aim. He just pointed toward the sound and squeezed the trigger. He felt the explosion of the gunpowder, felt the butt of the rifle grinding into his shoulder. The muzzle kicked up and he opened his eyes. The first thing his eyes registered was the bullet striking a tree. A miss. He began to slide the bolt to load another shot when his gaze fell upon it. Time, like his heart, seemed to stop completely.

It had the face of a man. This he knew, but this thing was of no earthly origin. Evolution had no hand in the Frankenstein amalgamation that met his gaze. Nor could he conceive of any god that would allow such a vile thing to touch its earth. Perhaps it wasn't; Earth. Perhaps, in the fog, he had crossed into another plane and this was some hellish dimension with no gods or kings; only monsters.

The stern face of the human head stood around seven feet off the ground and was connected at the back to a long, shaggy, muscular neck. The neck fed into the body of a deer, but the proportion of the torso was too unnaturally elongated, and the hind quarters of the beast drooped, like that of an old dog or a rat. Though strangely stretched, the body was powerful with lean muscles, their developed striations pushing against the tight skin.

The powerful frame stood atop four gangly, stilted legs. They were deer-like, covered with a brown coat of fine fur, until the hairs ended abruptly at four, calloused human hands with thick, yellow and dirt-covered fingernails.

Up one of the front legs was a long, grizzly burn scar. The long healed damage continued to trail all the way up the limb, across its chest, and up along the neck, leaving a swath of old scar, a landscape barren of fur.

In contrast to the fine, bestial hairs, the hair atop its head was long, straight, and black. The silken locks shone with a healthy sheen in the moonlight. The creature's braids hung down the sides of its head and dangled ever so gently with the slightest movement.

The head was in full view now, and for the first time he was able to take it all in. At a glance it could be mistaken for normal in all

164

measures, but exposed out in the open, the head, like so much of the creature, was just wrong. The jaw was oversized, exaggerated, and brutish. It rested just below the overly pronounced cheekbones, and was paired with an aquiline nose and a sloped forehead with a heavy brow. As he gazed at the horrendous beast, the feature that stood out the most was the elongated skull, giving the creature an extended cranium and an improper visage.

The entity stood there, unmoving and statuesque. The shot that he fired had whizzed inches past its head, but the abomination didn't so much as flinch. While Jay tried desperately to get the second shot into the chamber, the braids flicked up and branched like antlers to create a splendiferous, symmetrical formation atop its head. The innermost of the barbs on the antler-like structures seemed to come together to create a biconvex shape between them. A lens. An eye.

As the psychic lines of the third eye closed together to seal its shape, Jay felt suddenly *happy*. His fingers fumbled with the rifle, suddenly becoming quite uncoordinated. The thing from the mist slowly began to walk toward him. With each step it delicately raised its leg high and with a bent wrist. Then as it stepped down the wrist curled outward, the hand flattened and was delicately laid against the earth.

As it closed the distance, the quasi antlers swayed and seemed to almost jiggle and tense oddly. Seeing them as they neared, Jay was able to see that they were not, in fact, braids of woven hair. Upon the beings head sprouted two black tentacles with smaller protrusions that gave the illusion of prongs. They had hung limply, clutching the long strands of genuine hair that grew out from the scalp, which hung limply. Now, though, the midnight hued tentacles were flexed and tight, standing upright. The jet black hair was long and dangled beside the creature's face, swaying as it stepped ever closer, framing its murderous gaze with its disheveled strands. A faint yellow glow seemed to illuminate in the exact center of the third eye the antlers held. It thrummed warmly, brightening with each pulse.

Jay felt a warm feeling behind his ears and at the base of his neck. It was calming and he wanted nothing more than to just give in to the comfort and rest. He wanted to just lay on the earth and let the world pass him by, but there was something he wanted more than rest.

His dull hands had finally managed to fumble the slide enough to load a second round. The rifle lifted. The muzzle swayed as he fought to keep his eyes open and stay upright. He teetered, trying to use the tree at his back to stabilize. He had almost steadied his aim enough to let loose the second bullet, but the creature wouldn't allow it.

In a terrifying surge of speed, it lurched forward, spraying dirt and topsoil behind it as each of its powerful hands gripped the ground and launched the beast forward. It grabbed the muzzle and wrenched it skyward. The violent jerking was too much for his weary body, and it was torn out of his hands as the gun went off.

It was all Jay could do to keep his balance. The chimera towered over him. It stared down and held him with such a furiously intense gaze, that there was no hope for him to look away. All he could do was stare back, wide eyed. With a flick of its arm it tossed the rifle into the bushes while it continued to suffocate him with its intense, stern, yellow eyes. The grimace, ever present upon its face.

With a slow bend of its neck, it lowered its head and came face to face with Jay. It was so close he could smell its putrid breath and feel the hot air against his lips and cheeks. Its penetrating gaze bore into Jay's eyes as it simply said, in a long, drawn out growl, "Nnnnno."

Jay whimpered. It was the only course left to him. What could he do, but balk in the face of such power? Such strangeness. Its lips peeled back for a final time, unsheathing its enamel daggers, ready to rend his flesh off in chunks and mouthfuls. This time was different, though. The mouth opened wide, but there was more. Its mouth continued to stretch and its cheeks raised. It was smiling. It was smiling and then it began to laugh, deep within its long throat. It was an unnatural and husky thing to hear. Truly, it was like the pant of a dog with the malice of a man, a demon.

The complex torrent of emotions in Jay's mind felt like they were about to make his head implode. Terror in the face of death.

Revulsion at the jovial cannibal whose grasp he had willingly thrown himself. Sadness at a life wasted. Indignity at the realization his life was doomed from the start. But worst of all, he felt happy. Not just because of the steady drumming of the psychic sun that melted his muscles and made him feel like he'd been lobotomized, but because he was finally going to do *just one good thing*. Just one thing right in his whole. Fucking. Life.

He let go. His arms fell to his side, he was ready. His executioner lifted one hand up and grabbed his collar tight, crushing it with its vice grip. Then it pushed him hard into the tree and used him to pull itself up until it was grasping his collar with both front hands. It had stopped laughing, but it still wore a grin only fit for a devil. The hands slid up his body until they were around his neck. Then they squeezed.

As the fingers locked around his throat, Jay was reminded of the time he'd first met Tim. Tim had a handshake that could splinter wood, but the hands that found their way to his neck could pop stones into sand. Immediately Jay felt it; all of it. The crushing of the life from his body. The pressure in his face that caused it to turn beet red. The way his lungs tried to pull air, though the attempt was in vain. Darkness started to blur around the edge of his vision as his strangulation continued without a drop of mercy. In just a few seconds he would meet his end.

His arms fell to his side, limp. As they dangled, though, his fingertips brushed against something; a bulge on the side of his pants. He didn't know why this little distraction caught his attention so completely. Maybe he just didn't want to focus on the pain of his throat collapsing. More as an idle reaction than a conscious choice, his hand found its way into his pocket. It was the tiger handled knife. For a brief instant his animal mind glimpsed an escape. He managed to slip the weapon out and flounder the blade open just as his body went limp. His vision was black now. With his very last thought, he gripped the blade in his fist and flexed his bicep as hard as his failing body would allow.

He felt fur. Then he felt wetness, and warmth. Finally he felt pain. Pain indescribable. His mind felt like tissue paper in a blender. The very center of his brain was a mixture of a migraine and a jackhammer that radiated all the way out to his skin and bones. He could feel it in his stomach, his fingertips, his balls. He could feel each hair on his head and they were needles stabbing him from every conceivable angle. The darkness of his vision became white and he felt the thud reverberate through him as he collapsed onto the ground, knocking the last of his wind out. In a hazy blur, his vision returned for just a moment. Long enough for him to see the deer beast bounding into the fog soak forest, a tiger print handled knife buried deep into its chest. Then there was nothing.

Sixteen: Release

A thought. He had a thought, which meant he could think. That meant he was still, somewhere. Was this the afterlife? Was he in heaven? If he was, which one? Or were they all the same? He guessed it didn't matter because this clearly wasn't heaven; not with how much his body hurt. He managed to open his eyes, which was quite a feat considering they were almost swollen shut. He was sure he'd broken every blood vessel in his face. Did he have a concussion? Breath came in wheezes and spurts until he coughed, which made him double over and vomit from pain. Each heave felt like a sledgehammer bashing against his skull, then in turn, the pain would make him dry heave and wretch even more. Eventually he managed to break the cycle and get himself under some semblance of control.

All he could do was wipe his mouth and roll onto his back, trembling, while he attempted to breathe like a normal human being. The fog had dissipated, and now the moon was at its zenith. It was perched in the heavens, suspended up above by unseen forces. Its illumination was so intense that it cast dark shadows in the night.

Though the light was bright, it did nothing to outshine the stars. Before him the Milky Way flowed lazily from one tree topped horizon to the other. The twinkling light show that was the infinite cosmos was profoundly beautiful in a way he had never appreciated. Out there, way up past the birds, the clouds, and the sky, there was nothing; but also everything. Out in the space between things, was everything that wasn't here.

He didn't know why, but in that exact moment he turned his attention to one corner of the sky off to the side. He wasn't sure what he had actually seen just then. It only took an instant, but seeing the after image as he blinked convinced him that he *had* seen something. There had been a light. A spike of light as bright as the sun that blipped into existence for a fraction, of a fraction of a second. It seemed to shoot off from the earth toward the sky and disappeared amongst the billions of tiny lights. He wanted to ponder the nature of that strange light, but thinking made his head hurt. So instead he opted to just admire the unadulterated beauty of infinity.

After an unknowable amount of time, he had taken in his fill of the night sky and figured if he wasn't dead yet, it wouldn't be proper to just lay there and die now. It took several attempts and the aid of a tree to lean on, but after an excruciating amount of work and pain, he was able to stand. A large stick lay nearby and with tentative, deliberate steps he found his way over to it. With his stick in hand and the light of the night sun to guide him, he began the long, slow march toward camp.

He didn't know how long he had hiked. All of his attention was solely devoted to staying on his feet. Eventually he found a rhythm and his mind glazed over, allowing thoughts to flow freely through him. One of those thoughts that flitted so carelessly through his mind suddenly panicked him. If he had succeeded, and they had all made it to camp, then they would think he was dead and would have left by now. If that was the case, what was he doing? He had nowhere to go and no hope of returning to... home? Civilization? He had nowhere to go. Several moments passed while he mulled over the thought and what to do about it. If there was no hope for him, then why did his feet keep moving? Why? Did his body know something he didn't? After pondering the issue for another indeterminate amount of time he came to a conclusion. Sure, maybe he didn't have a way back, but the camp was familiar ground and from there he could carve out an existence. An existence just like the creature had. Well, maybe with less eating people.

With that, he looked up and found himself in an open clear cut. The terrain was muddy and compressed flat with tire marks and the treads of mechanical behemoths. Had the camp always been this uneven? He always remembered it being much more consistent and flatter. Though the earth was compacted, there were mounds and small hills and valleys in the features of the land. He could see where each bus had been parked in their lines. The food bus had left deep pits where the tires sat from the extra weight of food, appliances, and people shifting around in it while they cooked. The tables around the bus had left their own indentations as well.

170

Several bits of trash and debris were left where Mat's trailer had been broken into. The radio antenna lay broken and lifeless, half sunk into the mud and buried in dirt.

Looking around the empty field he didn't know where to even start. Then his eyes caught a glint of reflected moonlight. He turned his tired head to find the source, and upon seeing it, it made his heart swell and tears to trickle down his swollen, battered face. There, bathed in the light of the full moon, standing proud and majestic, was the biggest, most beautiful truck Jay had ever seen. Its blue paint shimmering and dancing playfully with the light. He hobbled over and took a peek through the window. The door was unlocked, and the keys were sitting on the seat. Dropping the walking stick he slid into the driver seat with a pained groan and just sat, taking it all in. With a wry little smile, he turned the key and listened to the engine roar to life. The earth-shaking transmission was so powerful, he swore it could be measured on the Richter scale. The headlights came on, and mercifully there was no wounded, nightmare abomination waiting for him. The truck circled around and with the sound of crunching gravel and a roaring engine, it began the long journey down the coiling mountain roads.

Epilog

The house was beautiful. Perhaps calling it a house wasn't *quite* accurate. It was really more of a small mansion, complete with a guest house, green house, patio, pool, and several other amenities of the moneyed. Mat walked up the long driveway toward the house. At the top of it sat a monstrous blue truck, standing proud, surveying the land like a watchdog. It was all uphill and as he approached, he could see a rather expensive looking telescope protruding from one of the upper windows. The garden was well manicured and was a lovely blend of function and form. It grew a gorgeous harmony of vegetables, fruits, berries, flowers, and decorative ferns and shrubs. It was a veritable micro-Eden and Mat would be lying to himself if he said he wasn't more than a little jealous.

As he reached the front door, Mat turned to look behind him. The world seemed to stretch out forever. Rolling mountains, like waves on the ocean, receded back into the landscape, each one becoming more lost to the horizon. Then behind it all, far off in the distance stood a squat, snow-capped mountain that grew higher than any other, and far beyond it stood a second with a pointed tip. Mt. Hood, he guessed. It was still morning and the low angle of the sun hit the snow in such a way that it made the mountains glow. The view was noble; breathtaking.

Eventually he tore himself away and rang the doorbell. A pleasant little tune met his ears and several moments later the door opened. Jay stood there with a tired, but content look in his eye. He was clean shaven, now, and his hair had grown out. It was done up and tied back into a messy bun. He was dressed in a simple grey tank top and black sweatpants. When he saw who was here to visit, his face lit up and without a word he launched into a massive hug. He tried, and failed, to lift the giant man off his feet.

Mat let out a deep chuckle. "Not quite yet, man. You're getting bigger though," he said, returning the embrace.

They released each other and Jay waved excitedly. "Come in, come in. What brings yah 'round?"

"We completed a season ahead of schedule, again. Zack's got the whole thing running smoother than a greased-up seal, so I thought I'd drive out, poke my head in."

They stepped inside and Mat took a moment to admire the interior. There was a central hall with open archways on either side leading to different rooms. It was lovely. Several paintings of landscapes hung from the walls. Small tables were strategically placed to fill in the space without crowding it. Upon the tables were decorative bowls, pictures and small potted plants. The hall was painted white with a very subtle light blue used as trim here and there. There were patterned reliefs above their head to add just a touch of visual noise to the hall. The bannisters were ornately hand carved from wood, each one was a stylized tree from the region.

At the end of the hall was a staircase that led to the second floor. A trail of various clothing items lead suspiciously up them. The two men stepped into the kitchen and dining room where the remnants of a meal for two still sat, along with more than a few empty beer bottles.

Jay rummaged around in the cupboards and asked, "Do you want some coffee? I just brewed a fresh pot."

"Yeah, I'll have a cup. Just a little creamer if you've got it. It's a cheat day. Looks like you didn't make it to dessert."

Jay set to preparing the drink. He looked confused for a moment, then glanced at the table. "Oh, yeah, me and Pharrell were, uh, up late last night."

Mat shot him a sly grin. "You dog."

Jay turned red and chuckled nervously. "So things are going good for you?"

Mat pulled up a seat at the kitchen island. "Yup. Honestly the hardest part is finding the land now. I'm thinking of changing over to hemp production. Zack's been going on about it and he's starting to turn me. Crazy fast production, more yield, more diverse portfolio, grows damn near anywhere. He even made a whole presentation about the cost efficiency, production techniques, and a layout of how we could convert our business without any layoffs.

The kid's damn smart when he sets his mind to something. I see you've been doing well for yourself," he said, spinning his finger around to indicate the home.

"Hell yes, brother. I've got a few things goin' 'round here."

Mat was handed his drink and they sat for a few minutes, just gazing out the window at the scenery while they sipped their mugs. After a while Mat put his mug down and looked over at his old friend. Jay looked back, puzzled, but didn't say anything. Mat gave him a concerned little smile and asked, "How are *you* doing? Have the dreams gotten any better?"

Jay closed his eyes and nodded, not to answer the question, but in his understanding of it. "Eh, there's nights he needs to wake me up 'cause I'm screamin' or thrashin', but yeah, they're few an' far between these days. You know, I don't think I ever thanked you."

Mat gave him a quizzical look. "For what?"

"For giving me the job, for leaving the truck, for backing up my story at the station. All of it. I know you're gonna say somethin' like, 'of course, you're my friend', or somethin' all gooey like that, but I mean it. I really appreciate everything you've done for me and I wanted to say thank you."

Mat grew a mischievous grin and leaned back with his mug. "Of course, I'll always look out for you. You still owe me four dollars and forty five cents. Can't have you squelching on our bet, now can I?"

As he took a sip, Jay accidentally snorted into his coffee, jumping a few drops onto his upper lip and nose. Laughing, he wiped away the spill. "Damn it, you're still doggin' me about that? I told you I'd get you back when my dadd'eh paid me my allowance," he said, chuckling into his next sip.

They laughed warmly for a bit. Then Jay got an excited look on his face and jumped up. He motioned for Mat to follow. "Oh, come'ear, I wanna show you somethin' I've been workin' on," he said excitedly, and hurried his friend up out of his seat and down the hall.

They entered a massive room with an entire wall made out of glass panels. Natural light poured in to reveal a painting almost the size of the two story wall it hung on. It was unfinished, but its shape was becoming clear. It was an idyllic landscape with rays of light piercing clouds to shine down on white mountains, green forests and mighty waterfalls.

Mat gave a long, slow whistle. "Who's overpaying you for *this* monstrosity?"

Jay looked at it with reverence, resting his hands on his hips. "It's for the corporate offices of some Fortune 500 down in Portland. They asked for a price, so I just spat out some high ball number thinkin' they'd haggle me down. Crazy fuckers just said 'yes' and broke out the checkbook."

Mat continued to drink in the massive artwork. After a few comfortable moments of silence he asked, "Did you put it in yet?"

"Yeah. S'up there on that ridge, there in a tree."

Looking where Jay pointed, Mat could see a deer barely visible in the dark shadows of the branches, its head bearing three dim circles for eyes with just a minimalist amount of yellow blended into the black paint to keep them obscured. It would have been essentially invisible if it hadn't been pointed out. "You know I was listening to some expert people talk about you on the radio coming over here. Once people noticed it, they went through all your old work with a fine tooth comb. They were calling it your 'second signature'."

Jay's response was a short hum of recognition, but Mat could tell he was beginning to spiral away. "I don't think you ever told me why you started painting," he said, trying to bring his friend back.

Blinking a few times he shook his head and began surveying the rest of the piece. "Well, I was bored out of my gourd goin' through rehab and I said as much to my therapist. She said I needed an 'outlet'. So I tried to pick up whittling again, but they didn't take too kindly to me laying around with a bunch of knives, choppin' up wood and leavin' splinters 'round. I liked the land 'round these parts

176

so that's what I painted. Then between the media attention around the camp, and my 'tragic backstory' people just started buying them; for too much money, I might add. Not that I'm complaining."

"So that's all you need to be an artist? Some paint and a sad start?"

Jay shrugged. "Worked for *me*."

They chuckled warmly and exited the room. While they walked down the hall Mat asked, "If you're pulling in that much, please tell me you're investing some of it."

"Oh yeah, yeah. I got a guy and everything. I put my money to work. The house is paid off. 'Course, now that it is, I don't really know what to do with it. I've never been the hoity toity type. I sent a bunch to the mother of, well, you know; *that* guy. I made it look like she won a contest. Di'n think she'd much like gettin' it from me. I donate a bunch of it, too. Phil-, phulon-"

"Philanthropy?"

"Thank you, that word. I do some of that. About an even mix of, keep kids in school, keep 'em fed, and the other half to helpin' convicts get back into the world; pay it forward an' all that. Then I pay just about nothin' in taxes because it's all written off. It's nuts the kinds'a things you can get away with; uh, legally, mind you."

They walked to the living room where a T.V the length of a couch was quietly tuned to the news. A still steaming cup of coffee rested, waiting on the table. "Ah, that's where I left you. Forgot my first cup when you knocked," Jay said, and scooped up the brown brew. They sat down and stayed comfortably quiet for a short while.

Then Jay piped up. "How's Earl and Tim doin' these days?"

Mat leaned back to get comfortable in his seat. "They're doing good. Tim's got a garage up and running, he works on specialty and vintage cars. Earl got interested in cooking while he was healing up, went to school for it and last I heard he's just opened his third restaurant. Even headhunted a few of my guys; the crafty SOB. No one could make mac and cheese like Greg, now I've got to pay for it."

Warm laughter ensued and the conversation wound on, long into the day, the television acting as pleasant white noise.

"-Yes, Tom, those are some cute puppies. Switching to local news, no word, unfortunately, on the whereabouts of those missing campers. Michel and Gregory Tambers went missing last week while backpacking in the Washington forests, north of Mt. Saint Helens."